House of Eden

YD LA MAR

EMERY LEEANN

Acknowledgments

I need to thank Yongda. She is so fucking awesome, always keeping me in line, which isn't easy. She had my back through this entire project, and I am so eternally grateful and excited that we were able to share this vision together! Fucking love your face woman!

I want to thank my amazing PA's, Samantha Lynn and Shanna Renee. Without them, no one would know who I am.

Also, a special thanks to my bestie Elizabeth St. John who always makes me feel good about my writing even when I don't feel good about myself.

I want to thank all of the reader's groups who continuously promote my work. Without you, I wouldn't be around.

And the readers, you all amaze me. When I get a message that says, Holy shit! I didn't see that coming! I'm still always in awe that people love my books. I fucking love you all so much for this.

And last, but certainly not least, my family. They have to hear me agonize over story lines and plots and word counts and edits and – well, you get the point. Lol. They are always there to lend me their ears and let me bounce my ideas off of them. Love you all.

~ Emery LeeAnn

∞∞∞∞

To my wonderful husband, who never bats an eye when I come up with crazy ideas, but instead just adds to it, making my stories come alive. My children, who tell me every day that they are proud of me.

To my beta readers. You guys are the real MVP. Thank you for sticking it with me through the initial phases of my writing journey. All of your feedback has inspired me to better myself and my writing ability. Tia, Selena, Jackie, Tiffany and everyone else who beta read, thank you for bouncing ideas with me.

To all my readers, thank you for giving me the chance. I hope I can continue to make you guys proud.

~ YD La Mar

Blurb

In this house, we do one thing.
We bring pleasure.
We serve the debauchery of others.
We are the masters.
When outside forces threaten to topple our empire,
We do the only thing we understand.
We fight back...with our bodies.

Tyrants, traitors and everything in between.
Nothing stands between the House of Eden and our goals.
The mortality of mothers, the fate of daughters.
Will this game of power ever end?

...it is we who supply
what is needed among
the commotion of necessity
yet sometimes we are
pushed to the extent of
what we never deserved
abused and misused
but only time will allow them to see
that it is we
who carry the burden
of every man.

YD La Mar

Prologue

ERDENE

"You all know why we're gathered here. I give you ladies simple rules, and one above all others. One!"

I hold up a black latex-gloved finger to emphasize my point.

Staring each of them in the eye, I memorize their worried features. Each girl, handpicked by me, were destined to join me in my army of Edens. Women who would fulfill the most depraved fantasies of both men and women. Yet, staring at them all right now, they're all worthless bugs under my shoe.

My stiletto heels continue to *click click click* with my every step across the basement floor as I pace in front of them. Those standing, shift nervously on their feet. The one on the table sobs softly. My irritation rises exponentially.

"Has a cougar caught everyone's damn tongue? What have I told you, ladies?" My voice bounces off the walls, the need to raise it in octaves grates on my nerves.

In unison, their voices echo back in the room. "We are Eden. The garden flourishes where genesis ends."

Click click click.

My heels snap down harder as my steps bring me closer to the one currently on her back, strikingly pale against the steel table she is strapped upon. The rules were so simple. She tests me, surely. Little does she know, I'm not the one to be prodded. No. That will be my pleasure now.

Bending over to look into her eyes, I watch with apathy as her tears flow down sideways, hitting the smooth metal beneath her. She hopes I will feel something akin to mercy. I feel nothing beyond cold fury.

"Cici. Your attempts to fool me into any sympathy is for naught. There will be no sympathy here. Haven't I shown you this? Haven't I shown all of you this, time and time again?"

My fingers, smoothed by the signature elbow-length gloves I wear as Mistress, trails along the spiked gag in her mouth; the crimson against the pale flesh of her cheeks is beautiful to look at. She was one of my best too, which angers me even more because now I have to find a replacement. I watch with dispassion as blood trails from the side of her mouth, the sharp spikes marring the once smooth skin.

"I feel like–" Keeping a calm front, I straighten myself back up without taking my eyes off her naked form strapped to the table. "–you test me. Or was this what you wanted all along? Have I pegged you wrong? Was pain your pleasure after all?"

The sound of shuffling behind me becomes background noise as I make sure to position myself in a way that every lady in the room will be able to witness the wages of Cici's sins in the House of Eden.

"I could have worked with that, you know." Pulling the dagger from the small table nearby; the blade glints against the light cast from the bulb overhead.

Cici moans against her gag, and I'm not quite sure if it's from pleasure or pain, not that it matters anymore. Walking along the backside of the table, dragging the blade along the way, I stop right beside her growing womb. Her skin is starting to become taught with how far along she is.

I should have kept a better eye on her. No. That is incorrect. One of the patrons should have informed me. *Men.* For all I know, it was one of their fetishes they wish to be kept hidden from the Madame of the house. Pregnancy is common in a whore house. It's not that fact that she conceived but the simple fact that she chose to hide it. Well, nothing goes on under my roof without me eventually finding out.

"Did you think you could hide for very long? Or did you want me to catch you, just like this?" My hands caress her, watching as the goosebumps rise on her skin from my touch. "To have my way with you?"

Turning my head toward hers, I watch as her eyes widen in fear. The organ inside of my chest beats steady as I lift my gloved finger to my lips to tell her to be silent.

"Hush, hush," I coo. "Make no sounds now."

My limbs are quick despite not having practiced in a while, not like this.

The swing down makes my heart beat loudly against my ears, pounding in tune to the moment the blade sinks into the belly button like a bullseye. Cici's screams make my lips lift into a grin as my breast starts to feel heavy. My blades are always maintained.

The slice of flesh creates little to no resistance as I carve at her skin downward toward her hip bone. The blood drips out in globs, filling the table before spilling over and landing on the floor beneath us in splatters. I press my legs together and suppress a moan. I've started to gravitate toward the macabre sight, inhaling its scent into memory.

A whimper from nearby ruins my moment. My face lifts toward its direction, my eyes narrowing to focus on what stole my attention from my task.

I catch my ladies scooting closer to each other, some with their arms around the other's waist as they try and twine their bodies into the background, to make them less noticeable. That simple fact makes my lip curl. Partly in amusement, partly in a sneer.

Seeking, seeking. They're always seeking. If they would just follow the rules, they wouldn't have the need for this weakness. I've trained my ladies to be proud of the attention they gather, to hold themselves high because it's the house they represent, not just themselves.

Yet, here we are.

Disappointment seeps into my very marrow the longer I stare at them. Reward and consequence. It's black and white. But there's always one who wants to paint it red. It's a good thing red is my color of choice as well when given the opportunity.

I slap Cici, and her eyes flutter back open. "I'm going to need you to keep your eyes on me, lovely. I do hate it when someone can't follow the rules of their Mistress."

Slicing upward, I let the blade guide me until it hits her sternum with a hard stop. The way her intestines spill out reminds me of opening my legs, waiting for pleasure, and it makes my nipples hard.

Someone gags, and another dry heaves in the background, making me frown. "Now, now. I know I've trained you girls better than this." Always disappointing. I'm going to have to start training them harder.

One of the girls grins and licks her lips at me, cooling my temper down. Möngömaa. She's been the longest in the house. I know I shouldn't pick favorites, but she's gotten under my skin with her work ethic.

Bringing my attention back to the task before me, I lay the blade down in the pool of blood, freeing my hands to pull back her skin. Ah, it seems the fetus hasn't fully formed yet–or was it my blade that sliced through its delicate neck and spine? Well, too late to cry over spilled milk.

My eyes glance at Cici, whose blank stare has clouded over, the blood from her gag dripping down her chin like cum in a cumdumpster. "Isla, bring me one of the jars."

"Yes, Mistress."

My nipples get harder from her address, beyond the cool temperature I keep down here in the basement. Though I'm known as the Madame of the house, there's just something about a slave calling its master by their rightful title.

The ambient gagging has stopped, but muted retches can still be heard. *Later, these ladies will be licking this floor clean*, I muse to myself. They will learn that some fluids are more welcomed than others.

I stand rooted, my eyes watching the sway of Isla's hips as she grabs my request off the shelf in the back. Isla turns around quickly and comes scampering back like a church mouse, her head bent down as she presents the item to me. Petting her head, I take the jar and turn, twisting off the top. My hands reach for the formaldehyde solution that's been pre-made on the metal shelf near me. Pouring in the solution about halfway, I call out for Isla again.

"Hold this."

Her hands shake but she does as she's instructed, her face turned toward the other girls rather than myself. I'll have to punish her for that later. All eyes must always be on me. I require undivided attention in moments like this.

I slowly pull the fetus out, careful to keep the little body as whole as I can and drop it into the jar. I smile as I seal it back up. "Isla, place it beside the others. Labeling it under her mother's name."

My gloves have proven pointless as the blood has stained

well beyond my elbows by now. Sighing at the extra cleanup that has to be done, I turn to my girls.

"That will be all for today. I will be checking up on each of you later this evening. Do not forget what we've all learned here. The ladies of this house are what keeps things running. If the order of the garden is disrupted, our empire falls, and you girls will be left to rot. I can guarantee, you will surely miss home in the House of Eden then. Am I understood?"

Their mumbled replies make my teeth grind. Narrowing my eyes at each of them, I ask again. "Am I understood, ladies?"

"Yes, Mistress."

I should have them all burned at the stake. How simple would it be to start over?

"Dismissed," I bark. "Make sure you all complete your nightly routines in preparation for tomorrow. There's no rest for the weary here." The girls start to line up behind each other in a single file as they exit up the stairs. "Möngömaa, you stay with me."

"Yes, Mistress."

When the girls have all disappeared, and none of their footsteps can be heard, I turn my eyes to Möngömaa.

"I tire of the stresses these girls put me through. Grab that piece there and prepare to please me." Not looking to make sure she follows my instructions, my hands skim along the soft flesh of Cici, now cooling on the table.

What a pity and waste. She really was a beauty, and brought in patrons that quickly became regulars in our house. I'm going to have to find out who let his seed grow in her, festering for his own pleasures. The thought of wringing his neck and slicing his dick off to shove in his mouth makes me tingle between my own legs.

Everything in due time.

Bending over, my mouth covers Cici's pert nipple, sucking

it to see if I can milk her the way she's milked one of the patrons. My body is bent over, leaning against her now cooling flesh, when hands push my pencil skirt up to my waist. I feel something firm press against my pussy. Moaning as it slides up and down against my wet folds, I bite onto Cici's nipples when Möngömaa shoves the strap-on inside of me to the hilt.

She begins to pound inside of me as my hands drag up the blood from Cici's abdomen and glide it against her other breast, squeezing and pulling. It shouldn't have to be this hard to keep these girls in line. Why can't they all be like Möngömaa? She always pleases me, especially when I need it most, like today.

The sound of wet flesh on flesh gets louder, the smell of my arousal filling the air and mixing with the smell of copper from the pooling blood. I try to hold tight, but my hands slip on the crimson coating table, slamming my head against Cici's breast and chest. Möngömaa pushes my head down firmly, thrusting until the pain between my legs starts to mingle with the pleasure. Her hands slap my clit, pinching and pulling until finally, I feel myself fall over the edge in ecstasy, moaning against Cici's now cooled, firm body.

When Möngömaa pulls the strap-on out of me, I can feel my own wetness dripping down the inside of my legs, arousing me again. Things are never simple, are they?

Standing up and straightening my skirt, I make sure my hair is still in place as my apathy washes back over me. "Möngömaa, make sure you put everything back where it belongs and clean up this mess. I don't want to have any trace of Cici here the next time I'm forced to come back down. Oh! As for the vomit on the floor, have the girls come back down and lick it up. Whenever you're ready. If they give you any protest, come get me."

"Yes, Mistress." Like the good little pet she is, she does everything I ask with a smile.

Chapter One

MÖNGÖMAA

The Mistress always trusts me with the jobs she needs done correctly. The other girls, truly, they try, but none can measure up to the chemistry we share.

I watch our devoted house servants remove the disemboweled body for disposal, then I work to finish cleaning all the congealed blood. It's a lot, but I don't mind. It's mindless work. When it's all said and done, everything is clean and the room smells heavily of bleach.

"Möngömaa?" A timid voice comes from behind me.

Turning around, I see a group of the girls. They know if they aren't turning tricks in the brothel, there is plenty of cleaning to do. Why they are wasting time hiding in the shadows is beyond me.

"Speak." I sound irritable, but this shy shit doesn't bode well with me. The girls know my philosophy. Time is money. The longer they keep me from finishing this task, the longer it'll take to have a cock shoved down my throat and coin in my pocket.

"We want to leave."

"Leave?" I scoff.

These girls can't live without this work. They will starve to death, not to mention they will lose all of the protection that Eden gives them.

"I'm glad you all are here. Mistress says you all are to lick up the vomit you spewed during her demonstration. I suggest you have the floor very clean for the Mistress' inspection. You do not want to anger her more."

I hear their gasps of alarm and shake my head at them. I don't feel bad. They should have known better than to pull that weak shit. This is not my problem.

I wash my hands and walk past them, knocking Isla back a step with my shoulder. Smiling at the little yelp that comes out, I point to the air around us. "Remember, someone is always listening, always watching. So do as you're told or suffer as Cici did."

With my chores done, I leave the basement and skip the rest of the way through the house.

Going toward the Botanical Room where Raj is waiting on me, I slip into the vanity to spruce up first. He tips well as long as I'm willing to keep his proclivities to myself.

Stripping down, the only thing I keep on my body is the strap-on. I rub rose oil on my breasts, and the phallus that is sticking out, ready for our session.

Knocking lightly, I enter the aromatic room. It's humid, with many botanical scents. Raj appraises me with his eyes, appreciatively. My payment is lying on the bureau, under his contract.

He is already on his back upon the bed, with his wrists in restraints and a ball gag in his mouth; thanks to the house servants who prepare the clients for their sessions. As I walk in, he lifts his legs up, ready to indulge in those things the servants know nothing about. I piggyback his ankles with each wrist so he looks like a trussed-up hog.

The lusty look on his face makes my nipples hard. The ball gag, where I will eventually plant myself tonight, is widening his jaw and stretching it out, readying his mouth to take my large strap-on when I fuck his face later.

I tap his sack, slapping a little harder each time. Back and forth, each globe bounces accordingly. Precum oozes out, glistening and beckoning me. Taking my tongue, I lick the very tip seductively, making him moan around the gag. His cock bobs, hitting me in the mouth. Moisture seeps from between my legs in response.

"Do you want extra lube?" I ask him.

He usually shakes his head no and this time is no different. There is always the hope he will change his mind, but he says he likes the burn - and truthfully, I like to watch him burn.

Repositioning myself, I align the head of my strap-on up with his rear entrance, plunging it in with one thrust. We both grunt at the same time. Purring, I use the restraints as hand grips to keep my balance, pounding him, until I feel his body quiver. Raj's eyes dilate the longer we connect and slap each other's bodies. Watching his ab muscles tighten, I know he is going to cum. Letting him release onto his stomach, I gently pull out of him when the pulsating dies down.

His breathing is heavy. The rise and fall of his chest, in addition to the sweat glistening, is mesmerizing. Climbing further up, I plant my seat on his face, rocking my exposed pussy on the ball gag stuck in his mouth. The strap-on bounces in the air above his forehead. He looks delicious under me, under my command. The firm pressure of his gag against my pussy lips brings my own pleasures higher and higher, the smell of sex increases in the room. My fingers swirl and pinch my clit with every grind, watching as his eyes stare at me in awe and worship.

It's this very fact that takes me over the edge, consuming me with shudders. Within minutes, I have his face soaking wet down to his chin. Can I get off by the intercourse? Absolutely. But any chance to rub my pussy all over someone's face, I'm going to do it.

It is all about control.

Removing myself, I fall beside him on the bed to catch my breath, letting him linger in wait just a moment longer. Unbuckling my strap-on, I toss it aside on the bed. When my heart slows down, I turn to release him. When I reach the lower part of the restraints, I smack him hard between his legs for good measure. Smiling in his direction, I stand and walk toward the main location to pick up my money.

Looking over my shoulder, I stare into his hungry eyes and tell him, "You are not allowed to come again until next week."

I hear, "Yes, ma'am," as the door closes behind me. He's just my first appointment of the day.

With his payment in hand, I make sure to count it twice before moving it into the safe I keep hidden behind the dresser back in my room. Raj is always one of my easier appointments. What a way to start the day.

In the House of Eden, you'll catch a glimpse of the strangest things in the hallways as us girls switch rooms back and forth according to our appointments. The hallway is decorated with maroon wallpaper, a testament to how old the building is. The lights give off just enough illumination for people to not trip. The area is sparse of any side tables or decorations as some of our clients like to come in and out quickly, just like my next client.

A loud knock on the door forces me to hurry and replace the dresser to its original position. With a quick side glance at my reflection in the mirror on the way to the door, I open it to find Mister Smith. His name probably isn't that at all, but at the House of Eden, we keep our client's secrets close to our bosom.

Stepping aside to let him in, Mister Smith is already stripping out of his jacket and business shirt. Closing the door, I walk over to the bed, already naked, and get on all fours the way he likes it. Every client has their thing, and the regulars usually like it the same way.

I can hear the sound of his footsteps as he goes toward the bureau to leave his payment. No electronic paper trails for Mister Smith. He makes sure of it.

The jingle of buckles and a soft whiz in the air is the only warning I get when his belt comes across my ass with a hard *thwack!* Biting my lip to hold in the cry, Mister Smith starts to breathe harder behind me as he runs his warm, wet tongue across the welt he's created. I've come to love the fine line between pain and pleasure, my past with the house clouds my emotions toward the two feelings. We are conditioned to not know the difference.

This fucker, Mister Smith, loves feeling in control whereas Raj is the exact opposite. I don't mind it either way. I am here as a vessel for their pleasure. Finding my own during their debauchery is a plus.

Thwack!

Thwack! Thwack!

I wriggle with every hit, the sting throbbing on my skin. My mind starts to feel floaty in the moment, an ascent to subspace.

"Turn around." His voice is gruff.

Doing as he says, I turn around to sit on the edge of the bed. Each movement of muscle makes the welts throb. My eyes look up to his in obedience right as he slaps my face with his hard cock, the wet feeling of his precum sticky on my cheek.

"Open up, whore."

We've played this game before. When I don't reply back, he slaps me on the other cheek with the palm of his hand.

"Yes, Sir." I whimper.

"That's it, suck it just like that. Take it like the slut you are." Like all the other times, the glint of Mister Smith's wedding ring catches my eye.

I wonder how he treats his wife at home, or if he bothers to ever go home.

"I'm going to cum in your mouth, and you're going to swallow every fucking drop, you hear me?"

This guy never lasts. It's sad really.

"Your pussy isn't good enough to take my dick. Suck. Just like that."

I discreetly stare daggers at his shaft, but continue to moan like I love everything he's doing to me.

When he bites his lip and his thrusts become erratic, I know he's close. He releases into my mouth, and I make sure to make a show of it dribbling a bit out the sides like he's offering so much when really, he's pathetic–just like most of the men who come in here.

But we are the House of Eden, we turn no one away from our garden.

When Mister Smith is done squeezing and shaking the rest of his cum out all over my face and lips in some show of prowess, he gets dressed without another word and leaves the room. *Thank goodness he cums quickly.*

Getting up, I walk back over to the bureau to count my payment. The good thing about our Mistress is, she provides us with good sized rooms with our own private restrooms. Well, my room anyway.

And this is exactly why it's good to be in her good graces.

I quickly go to the safe to deposit my newest earnings. I place the money into a tin box I use for the day's wages, hiding it back in its location before getting up to walk myself to the restroom. Sticking my finger down my throat, my diaphragm spasms and I regurgitate everything Mister Smith gave me. Wouldn't want to be filled up by everyone who wants me to swallow. It's something most of us girls have come to learn over time.

Washing my face, I hear another loud knock on my door. Drying myself with a towel, I quickly take a glance in the mirror to make sure evidence of my last client has been eliminated. Still naked, I walk across the room to see who it could be.

Swinging the door open, I see our Mistress standing there in her signature black satin robe, corseted tightly at her waist; the slit from her hip toward the bottom showcasing her long legs in sharp stilettos.

She's the perfect image of a femme fatale. Her scent is one that lures you in with a false sense of security-the light floral smell of something that makes you curious. We've come a long way together, having worked side by side for the past six years. But it's the Mistress' cunningness that got her to the top. Blood, sweat, and tears as they say. The Mistress has done it all to ensure our safety here.

I can respect that.

I also loathe it to my very core as I stare at the grin on her face.

"What can I do for you, Mistress?"

Her face doesn't change. Her eyes are sharp. "A new client has joined us and I want him to have the best experience, so I'm sending him to you."

Of course the bitch is.

"Is there anything I need to know beforehand?" It would just be my luck to have–

"I told him the hard limit is *death*."

Holding in my sigh, I plaster a false smile on my face as I

nod my head toward her. There's a sparkle in her eye, a hunger, for *what* I don't know. How far can you climb when you're already at the top with an army of whores beneath you to do your every bidding?

"Yes, Mistress."

"That's a good girl." She smiles with only her eyes, her lips stoic as she turns and walks away, her robe billowing behind her like the queen she is.

Chapter Two

ERDENE

Marching down the hallway, my ladies are all waiting inside their rooms for their next client. Some of the doors are closed, letting me know they're in the middle of a session. *Good.* Every woman in this house knows that time equals money, and we've worked too hard to get where we are today.

Another client has come into our midst, one with particular tastes for blonds. Stopping in front of Magda's room, my fists knock loudly on the closed door. The sound of flesh on flesh and carnal moans filter through before a masculine cry of ecstasy.

In less than five minutes, the door opens to reveal a disheveled male exiting the room, the smell of mixed bodily fluids permeating the air. My girls know every trick in the book to make a man finish when there's business to be had.

With her dirty blond hair strewn everywhere, Magda clasps her hands in front of her nakedness as she stares at my neck. "Yes, Mistress?"

"I have a new client for you. Special request. Client asked for a blond and who better than my little Magda?" There are others, but she's been a favorite among newer clients.

"Yes, Mistress. Is there anything I need to know?" My girls are good at schooling their expressions.

"Treat him well. He gave the house a sizable deposit for our lips to be closed about his presence. Anything you hear must go in one ear and out the other. Anything he wishes, you give. Anything suspicious, you come directly to me. This is going to be his trial period."

"Yes, Mistress."

"Good. He'll be up in five minutes."

With a nod, Magda rushes back into her room to get cleaned up and ready for her next appointment. Turning around and clapping my hands twice to get the attention of the girls with their door open, I make the announcement.

"High profile client. Shut your doors within the next two minutes. You can open them ten minutes after you hear Magda's door shut. Understood?"

"Yes, Mistress."

Like clockwork, each door starts to shut in succession until the only one left is Magda's. The head of his men coming up the steps are who I see first, their eyes going to my exposed thighs. With a seductive smile, I blow them a kiss as Mister Spence, as he told us to call him, comes up behind.

Broad build, the man looks to be in his early fifties, as he walks past me with a smile. My hands wave him into Magda's room. Magda is already sitting demurely on the bed - the picture of the perfect high-paid whore. We cater to all socioeconomic backgrounds here, to all flavors of debauchery and the clients know it, which is why they seek out membership and are willing to get on the waiting list if necessary.

Mister Spence has been waiting for two years, all his bribes proved useless to move him up the list. It might be the sadist in me because I enjoy watching him squirm and continue to try to use his power against me in a place where he has none.

Pressing my lips together, I watch as Magda closes the door behind him, his men standing outside the door like sentries. Keeping my thoughts to myself, I proceed like the sight doesn't make my gut churn.

"See you later, boys." A finger swipe on one collar, a caress on the cheek of the other, their eyes bore into mine with hunger. *Good.* Crave what you can't have gentleman because that's exactly how I'll be leading them by the balls if I need to.

Walking downstairs to the main lobby, I check on the girl I have behind the welcome desk. After all, we are a professional establishment in this area.

"Jessi, keep everything in order while I'm gone, would you?"

Her mousy brown hair moves with her as she nods her head in answer. "Yes, Mistress."

Walking toward the back office adjacent to the front desk, I continue to the other door on the back wall that leads to my own private entertainment room. Sometimes, we get clients who request the *Mistress* of the house. Who am I to say no to their money?

"Have you been a good boy while I was gone, Mister Jones?" I purr.

"Mmmmfmmmm."

Thwack!

"MMMMFFFPHH!"

Leaning in, toward his face, his pupils are dilated from his lust. His brows damp with a light sheen of sweat. *How long has he been struggling*, I wonder. "Hasn't your mother ever told you that it's not polite to speak with your mouth full?"

His eyes are pleading as they stare into mine. He does

nothing for me, but I play the game he wants me to play. My hands reach over, grabbing his balls and twisting them until his cheeks turn red from arousal. The sound of his cock slapping against his stomach is loud - begging to be touched, but I won't give him the satisfaction.

Leaning in closer, I lower my voice against his ear knowing full well his eyes are glued to the cleavage in front of his face. "If you're a good boy, I'll let you have a taste. But until then, I think I'll play with your *wife*."

Like that, I lean back and watch as his cock leaks, filling the air with a stronger smell of his arousal. *Naughty boy*. Turning toward the far corner of the room, the woman on her hands and knees inside the metal dog kennel hasn't said a word. She waits obediently, her eyes tracking my every movement. The weight of the chains connected to her collar makes her strain to keep her head in the correct position.

Taking my time, I torture her with how slowly I approach her little safe space. Her eyes sparkle and her hips shake with excitement as my hands reach toward the top. Unlocking the cage, I lead her out, still on all fours, to her husband who's chained to the bed, spread eagle.

"At least one of my pets has been good." Undoing her chain leash, I shove her face toward her husband's crotch, watching as she slurps and sucks his dick like the feral beast she is. I watch with fascination as her husband's hardness goes down with every swipe of her tongue.

See, Mister Jones has a specific appetite - an appetite for women of the Asian variety, which his wife is clearly *not*. Watching her dark hair move up and down, he groans from frustration as his eyes continue to stare into mine, begging, pleading, while I start to untie my silk robe before him.

The sound of his wife's moans lets me know that his cock is

coming back to life with what he sees. We'll see how long that lasts. Grabbing the hilt of my blade from the garter on my thigh, I walk up behind Mrs. Jones and caress the meat of her ass with the palm of my hand. She wriggles like a little puppy wagging her tail, silently begging for me to fuck her as her husband begs me to make her stop with his eyes.

"Good pets get rewards, Mister Jones." My hands grab and knead at the flesh before me, teasing Mrs. Jones into relaxing her body.

The moment it does... *Thwack!*

A red handprint starts to bloom against her pale skin and it makes my mouth water. I stick the hilt of my blade into her pussy, coating it with her juices. She whimpers, thrusting back to take more of it in. *Greedy little kitten.*

Can't have her getting what she wants so easily, now. Quickly removing it from her entrance, I flip the blade until the hilt is in my grip and shove the blade into her ass, cutting her flesh. Her screams are music to my ears as I continue to thrust in and out, in and out even after her body falls onto her husband's chest. Having trained her to be the good pet she is, she doesn't fight as my blade mutilates her back entrance, creating a wet crimson pool beneath her.

"Such a good little pet." She whimpers but doesn't stop me. When the fun dies down and she passes out, I push her off the bed with a thud and climb over Mister Jones until I'm straddling him.

Removing the gag from his mouth, I watch and listen as he sputters and coughs. Fucking myself with the same hilt of the handle, his mouth drops open watching me mix his wife's red tinged juices with my own as my hips start to grind down.

"Please, please." *Oh, he begs so prettily.*

"Mmmm, what are you begging for, pet?"

"Please. I-I-I need to fuck you."

"That's quite a problem you have, since this knife is doing a better job than you ever can."

"Please, Mistress!" It fascinates me how the depraved find themselves here.

Mister Jones, for example. His wife is probably bleeding out by the ass but his mind is in such a lust haze for me that he ignores the fact.

Groaning on the next inward slide, my voice becomes guttural. "What would you do for me?"

"Anything. Please! Anything!" *That's all I needed to hear.*

"Open your mouth." Crawling up to his face, I watch with glee as he eagerly does exactly as I ask him to.

In the house of Eden, one must expect the unexpected in order to play and win.

My blade slices the side of his cheek in a quick swipe, right before I lower my wet pussy on his face. Like the puppet he is, he only hisses from the pain but starts to devour me like a starved man, probing my pussy with his desperate, wet tongue. Oh, I have plans for Mister Jones, first son of Alexander Jones - The head business mogul of the biggest brothels in this city alone.

The fool beneath me has no talent whatsoever with his tongue, leaving me a little bereft. No wonder I left him tied up for so long. Shoving his forehead back with the palm of my hand, I crawl backward over his still restrained body and start to grind down against his hard cock. The blood seeps from the side of his lips onto the pillow but his eyes never leave me. Using the head of his cock to grind against my clit, I squeeze our bodies together until I find my release with no help from him. His groans tell me he loves the fact that I make him suffer. My hands make quick work on his shaft, gripping it harshly up and down, making him cum on his own chest before I leave the room to clean myself up.

I'll release him in the next thirty minutes, once his mind comes back to reality and he signs the contract I'm about to give him.

Chapter Three

MAGDA

Mister Spence has been sitting in the stuffed armchair since his arrival. The tension from the unknown spikes a bit of anxiety. Fixing his stare on me, he finally motions me up with his two fingers. Wanting to make a good first impression, I quickly comply, waiting for him to give me his next command.

This is the hardest part of getting a new client. Not knowing what they prefer. Once their routine is down, when they arrive, I'm already ready for them and there is no need for instructions unless they want to change it up a bit.

"Spin around," he pauses, "slowly."

He clearly wants to see what he was paying for. No problem since I have a regimented workout routine every day, not to mention all the calories I burn with my clients.

I can feel his eyes burning into me as I spin around slowly for his perusal. When I stop, he commands, "Crawl to me."

Dropping on all fours, I make sure to stick my ass out for his viewing pleasure. Since he doesn't reference either way, I take a chance and make a last minute decision. Making sure I sway my lower half with every move, I keep eye contact the whole way.

He leans forward in his chair with his elbows on his knees. Looking up to his face from my position beneath him, he places a hand under my chin. It's such a nice gesture that I can honestly say, I don't see his fist coming from the other hand until I'm already on the ground. The sting from the pain begins to throb and it feels like my cheekbone might have cracked. *It's never hurt this much before.* My face continues to pulse with pain as I try to push myself up with both hands against the ground.

The sharp sound of his voice breaks the silence in the room. "Stupid bitch, did I tell you to look me in the eyes?"

This high and mighty fucker right here.

I don't give him a response, remembering the Mistress' words about this man being a high paying client. I'm pretty sure I'm going to have a huge bruise on my face from the swelling I can already feel. He doesn't let me dwell in my thoughts long when he grabs my hair and starts dragging my body across the floor, making my scalp scream with pinpricks of pain, and throws me on the bed.

"Apologize. Now." He barks.

One of those types, huh? I play his stupid little game in hopes of making this appointment end quickly.

"I'm sorry, Sir." I mumble.

My scalp is still on fire from being manhandled. Tears are leaking out the corners of my eyes and it makes me feel weak. I don't like it. I'm not sure what is happening or what to expect from this guy, so I throw out the *safe word*.

"Polynesia."

In all of our contracts the patron signs, they know if the girl says the safe word, the guest has to stop and let the girl explain what the issue is. If there isn't a chance that both sides are agreeable to restart then they have to call the Mistress in and let her mediate. That has never happened before, especially *not for me*. It's usually a common misunderstanding with one of the new girls who feels better after having the act explained to her.

Shit, I've been here for years and this is the first time I've had to use the safeword.

I put my hand up, and repeat myself. "Polynesia."

He looks at me in disgust. "Are you fucking kidding me? You are supposed to be a professional."

I try to keep my face stoic. *Is this fucker kidding me?* He's the certified asshole that starts going nuts for no goddamn reason.

"Sir, I'm only using the safe word for an explanation. Could you please explain your plan for our session? I did not read your contract, which is in my right. However, the Mistress does not usually allow her staff to be marked. I just want to be prepared." I'm lying out of my ass, but he doesn't know that.

I just want to get rid of the guy.

My look of resolve must convince him. Or so I thought. Judging by the ugly sneer on his face, I'm lying to myself.

"And I also notice, you have not laid your payment out yet, which is another rule, payment comes first." This is not something I pulled out of my ass - this is something I know *for a fact*.

I have no qualms when it comes to money, since my body isn't free. People pay, get their service, and get the fuck out - a business transaction.

He growls and I can't understand what he says under his breath. But he does stand up to throw a wad of bills on top of the dresser.

"There you go. I wouldn't want to break your *rules*. My plan is to do whatever the fuck I want to. Your cunt of an owner said I just couldn't kill you. So, from what I can see," he looks at his watch, "you are my whore for the next forty-five minutes."

Lucky me. My mind is mentally choking him with that pretty watch of his but I keep my features schooled.

I must not do a good job because he catches me by surprise again. I want to ask if he'd read through the details of the contract. I want to ask if he preferred any certain position. Hell, I want to ask if he liked lingerie. So many things I want to ask, but his pummeling fists to my stomach stops me from voicing anything but grunts and screams.

"Ahhh!"

Each punch feels like my guts and organs are about to come out of my throat - bruised and tenderized from the inside out. Yet he dares to glare at *me* when I cry out in pain like I'm offending his piece of shit sensibilities.

The evil smile plastered on his face accompanies each successive hit.

My cries die down to whimpers as his fists begin to taper off as well. He sneers right up against my face, his hot breath making me want to vomit. Or maybe that's my guts wanting to physically escape.

"Good talk," he chuckles.

We are a whore house. Here to make the client's fantasies come true. Sexual fantasies usually. Sometimes they are rough, sometimes they are not. This man was beyond a sadist - a straight woman beater.

His hands grab mine and jerk me around, trying to restrain me as I kick and fight with all the strength I have left. I need to get out of here. I need to get away from this psycho. The Mistress wouldn't condone this - I refuse to believe it. But he is bigger and so much stronger than I am physically. I feel like my arms are being pulled out my sockets as Mister Spence throws me onto the bed unceremoniously. His body covers mine to hold me down so he can attach my wrists to something. I don't want to be in a disadvantaged state. I continue to kick and scream but a fist to my face stuns me.

Once he's done, he leans in with a voice full of menace, whispering into my ear, "Even if you could get away from me, my men are standing guard at the door."

My eyes widen at the fact. Would the mistress really allow that? Why do they need to stand outside the door? He's right. The realization that I'm going to have to endure this abuse hits me in the gut stronger than he ever could. Even if I continue to yell and scream, the other girls will assume I'm role-playing. My mind starts to become a little bitter toward the Mistress for sending this fucker my way. I wouldn't sentence any of the other girls to this kind of behavior.

Taking a knife out of his pocket, the glint of the blade makes me whimper before it morphs into screams.

"Ahh!"

He begins to slice pieces of skin off of my leg and my mind temporarily blanks out. The shock of what I'm seeing slows the pain from registering completely. Continuing to stare at him in disbelief, everything moves in slow motion as the horror of the situation finally brings me back to reality.

"Ahhhhh!!" A scream erupts out of me again like a volcano, right as he shoves a towel in my mouth. "MMmphhhh!"

One cut isn't enough, no. I scream bloody murder behind the towel as he cuts three more pieces off my leg. My head feels light, detached. I think I'm going to pass out but I don't. Instead, I'm forced to watch as Mister Spence sits back down on the chair in front of me and eats my raw flesh one piece at a time.

I waver from wanting to gag and wanting to pass out. The tears from the continued pain still radiating from my wounds clouds my vision. I try to blink it away but the feeling is too excruciating; the tears refuse to stop escaping.

At this point, my mind is in a weird haze. The rational part of it is trying to convince me that I didn't see what I just saw. I'm going crazy. Maybe I am dreaming. This can't be real, right? I'm almost convinced by my own thoughts until I see him coming back toward me with a demonic look in his eye. *Get away from me!* Of course he can't hear me. Ignoring the plea on my face, he sticks his thumb inside one of the cuts and presses down.

"MMMPHHH!!! MMMMMMMPH!" My anguished moan is muffled by the towel in place.

"You whores are all alike. You think your pussy is worth its weight in gold, when, in reality, it's not even worth the dung on the bottom of my shoe."

I've heard enough of that kind of talk growing up to not let it hurt me. But right now, vulnerable from the pain that still courses through my body, his words hit me like venom. I don't realize my eyes have closed until the sound of his footsteps echo around the room, making me paranoid. Trying to concentrate on dulling the pain mentally, I suddenly hear the swish of the cane before I feel it.

Thwack! Thwack Thwack!

"Mmmmphhh!" How much can one scream behind a towel before their voice leaves them?

My pussy is on fire.

Thwack! Thwack! Thwack!

My mind is lost in a different plane, in a subspace from reality as he continues to bring the cane down between my legs like I've offended him in a previous life. The menacing smile on his face with every hit makes him look like a demon from hell - maybe he is. He looks possessed.

Minutes pass, feeling like hours, and it feels like I'm floating outside of my body looking down on what's happening. *Thank goodness for small mercies.* Does he think he's punishing me for all the wrongs he thinks whores have committed and getting off on the fact at the same damn time?

Judging by the smile on his face after every hit, and every scream, I assume so.

I don't know how long my mind floats in subspace but things go blissfully dark, removing me from the overload of sensations I feel all over my body. *A small reprieve.* I'm harshly brought back to reality when my nostrils are assaulted by the strong smell of ammonia.

This evil man wants to make sure I feel every ounce of degradation and pain.

The smell of rose oil in my room, something that usually soothes me, right at this moment is nauseating. Glancing over with heavy lidded eyes, I look to see why he opened it. I witness him lubing his hand with the oil and my fear spikes. What else is he going to do to me? Was eating my flesh not enough for his entertainment? Walking toward me with ominous steps, Mister Spence stands over me like a reaper of death with his hand balled into a fist. He's already such a large man to my size but, in this position, it feels even more evident.

I know what is happening but a part of me still refuses to believe it. The denial part of my mind needs to be cut out because the pain of his large fist entering my pussy makes the pain from his caning feel like child's play. The swelling of my labia doesn't help matters either as Mister Spence continues to wedge it inside of me. My pelvis feels like it is going to explode from the invasion, the feel of the stretch to my body's maximum capacity. But, of course, this evil bastard can't just end there.

To add insult to injury, the thumb of his other hand manip- ulates my clit, forcefully eliciting some pleasure with my pain.

My mind is put in such a confused state from everything he's doing that I don't see the orgasm coming until it hits me, squeezing his hand and forcing the space between my legs to periodically go tighter. I truly have never been in so much pain as I am in now. Mister Spence doesn't stop fist fucking me, instead, forcing my body to ride the waves of my climax.

Pain and pleasure - pleasure and pain. Everything is becoming muddled, my body doesn't feel my own, my mind wanting to escape again but I can't.

Knock. Knock. Knock.

His time is almost up. Thank heavens there is some sort of mercy out there. Mister Spence lets out an exasperated sigh as he removes his fist from my vagina to walk over to the adjoining restroom sink.

The sound of water becomes soft background noise as I lie here, trying not to move a muscle. I can't tell if the throb between my legs is more from the residual orgasm or his fist tearing into me. The water turns off, telling me he's done. My body tenses up in anticipation of what else he might do to me on his way out. I can feel the weight of him depressing the bed, his shadow looming over me like the grim reaper once more.

"You are mine, dirty little cunt," he snaps.

What the hell does he mean by that? I'm a whore. I belong to the house.

"Mmmmphhh!!" The sting on my wounds makes me cry out again, biting down on the towel.

My eyes watch as Mister Spence holds his cock to continue pissing on my wound like an acid bath. The warmth of it on my exposed and opened flesh doesn't dull the pain as one would think. The pain is jarring enough to want to split my mind in two. Everything that's happened since Mister Spence entered my room is beginning to ebb and meld together, my world is drowned in fire.

With that evil glint in his eye, he moves so that his cock is aimed at my face. Turning my head to protect myself, he forcefully grabs my chin and pulls out the towel, tossing it onto the bed.

"Open that little whore mouth of yours." His commanding tone is final.

Shaking my head, he throws a fist to my face and I see stars.

"I said open up," he growls.

What am I to do under his power like this? I'm still tied to the bed with no escape. He pinches my nose and I'm forced to open my mouth for air giving him the chance he needs to spray me with his golden shower.

"Swallow it, now."

I have no choice. He won't let go until I do.

Knock!

He pats my face like I've been a good girl and leaves me to see himself out the door. Without bothering to turn around, he stands at the exit beside his men and speaks like he wasn't the devil that just ripped my soul out.

"Goodbye darling, I'll be sure to request you again."

The sound of the door closing is like a tomb, sealing me in alive.

Chapter Four

ERDENE

Mister Jones is a simple tool.

His father? Now that's a whole different beast.

Sitting in his prestigious office in the middle of the city, with my bare legs crossed in the tightest dress I own, my eyes glide over his tidy and sterile decor. So much control.

"Miss Ganbat, to what do I owe the pleasure?"

His presence is heady. He has an aura of dominance and menace making you want to be at his feet with just a glance of his stormy gray eyes. Unfortunately, for him, I've practiced the same entrance millions of times.

"Mister Alexander Jones. Your reputation does proceed you, as you know. What other reason would I have for a meeting?" Switching the weight of my body to my other hip, I make sure to cross my legs over slower than necessary.

His eyes track the movement from his seat behind the mahogany desk. *There it is. A simple male after all.* My insides purr at his reaction. He slowly leans onto his elbows and laces his fingers together, concealing half of his face.

"And what reputation might that be?"

"That you're a man with great power." Best to rub the ego to start out. Pet him like the good boy he is.

"And what kind of power would it take for a man like me to convince you of my prior proposition?"

My head tightens at the mention of our last meeting, but I keep a calm smile on my face. Life is a game and any slip gives your opponent an advantage. It's a proposition I will never take - I will never sell the House of Eden. It's become the heart of who I am, the heart of all the girls - *our sanctuary.*

Crossing my arms, I make sure to push my best assets forward for his viewing. "It seems today, I've come to *you* with a proposition of my own."

His eyes blaze and his nostrils flare, but he remains stoic as he lowers his arms onto the table, continuously staring into my soul from the other side of the desk. "Miss Ganbat, I'm not sure you are in *any* position to be offering *me* propositions. From what I remember-"

"-From what you remember, I didn't have this." As I stand, I pull out the slip of paper I had behind me while I was waiting for him to grace me with his presence. Making sure I bend over at the waist until he can get a good view of my cleavage, I slowly open the paper and slide it over to him with a wink.

His eyes never leave my breasts as he clears his throat and finally moves his gaze down to the piece of paper. It's when his frown turns into a sneer that I lean over and grab his tie, pulling him toward me with a kiss on the lips.

With a teasing lick against the seam of his mouth, I whisper against his lips. "Seems you've made sons with the same tastes. It's been a while since I've felt you between my legs, Alexander. Have you missed me the way I've missed you?"

He rips his tie out of my grip making me laugh softly.

"You need to get the fuck out of my office." His controlled demeanor only makes me hotter in this game we're playing.

"Or what, Alexander? Or you'll send your men after me? By the way, how is your wife doing?"

His nostril flares again, making me genuinely smile even wider.

"I think some of my girls caught your son stepping out of my quarters too." Batting my eyelashes, I force my smile to become demure.

He abruptly stands up and knocks his chair down, leaning toward me with fire in his eyes and menace in his voice. "What, Miss Ganbat, are you asking of me? Quit dancing around the subject and *spit it out.*"

He can be so attractive when he gets riled up like this, but I won't make his head too big. No, if anything, my dear Mister Jones needs to be brought down a peg or two.

"Oh, well if that's how you're going to be, you know what I want. A sizable offer might make me *forget* some things."

"Two hundred thousand and never come back here again."

"Alexander, with all the times you and your boys spend at the House of Eden getting your rocks off, I'd think you owe me much more than that. Your wife still hasn't found out yet or even suspects anything of her devoted husband. As for your daughter-in-laws... well-" He bares his teeth at me, grinding it down audibly as he slowly blinks. "-who's to say they wouldn't let the word slip to the Missus at their next shopping get-together, hmm?"

Turning around, I pretend to stretch my back by arching it, sticking my ass out for emphasis. Grabbing my phone out of my purse, I start to scroll through my contacts, stop, and look over my shoulder right before biting my bottom lip.

"Well, lookie here. Seems one of your sons must have connected his contacts with mine because here's your wife's number." My finger moves to make the call when Mister Jones aggressively wrestles it out of my grasp. The phone flies out of my hand and lands somewhere with a thud on the carpeted floor as we both continue to push, pull, slap, smack, and elbow each other for dominance of the situation. Alexander stands a head taller than my five-foot-six frame and he uses that fact to gain the advantage by pinning my hands behind my back, turning me and slamming my face onto his desk. He can be seductively rough when he wants to be. We're both panting, his chest presses against mine with every deep breath he takes. Pushing my legs together, I try not to give him the satisfaction of knowing how he's affecting me.

"Three hundred thousand, Erdene." His voice has become gravely as it whispers behind my ear. I see I'm not the only one who's affected by our little primal display.

"What the hell is that supposed to do, Alexander? Buy my girls new panties?"

He growls into my ear, the vibration of it going straight down between my legs, as his hips start to thrust against me suggestively. It's always been like this between us. Since the first day, years ago. He was newly married then.

"What do you want from me, Erdene? What are your goals? To take me down? For what purpose? You wouldn't be able to blackmail me anymore, then." His nose is grazing the back of my neck, giving me goosebumps.

My voice comes out breathy but I need to stay focused on the task. "Five hundred thousand."

"Five hundred thousand and-" His hands quickly pull up my dress. His voice groans into my ear the moment he finds out I haven't been wearing panties this whole time and the tussle we had earlier got me going - wet and ready.

The sound of his zipper going down makes me grit my teeth in anticipation. He's not the best I've had and he's not the worst, I've only been using the sex as leverage over him. I need to upgrade some stuff at the house and Alexander is the perfect man to shell out the money since he owns more than enough whore houses in the area.

Without any preamble, Alexander shoves his dick inside of me, the stretch he gives me making me lightly moan against my better judgment. His hips begin to pound like he hates me - and he probably does - especially the fact that he can't stay away from the House of Eden. I work my skills, clenching my pussy and pushing back against him to counter his movements, getting him to his finish as quickly as possible. The sound of our wet flesh hitting each other echoes in his office. My hands fondle his balls from between my legs just the way I know he likes it, from all of our time together, making him groan.

As usual, he pulls out and cums all over my ass, spreading it like he owns me when, in fact, he's got it twisted.

Pulling my dress back down, I grimace at the stickiness but school my features into a seductive smile. The satisfaction in his face tells me everything I need to know.

"The money will be in your account by the time you get back to the House of Eden. I hope to never see you again, Erdene."

Turning on my heels, I grab my things and walk toward the door. With my fingers on the handle, I look over my shoulder with another wink. "That's the thing about hope, Alexander. Hope can be *very* dangerous."

Chapter Five

MAGDA

Lying there, in and out of consciousness on the bed, the thought of never waking up isn't a horrible one. It's not that I hate my life. On the contrary, I adore making men's fantasies come true. There is a power behind it. A kind of force that flows through your body, making you feel invincible.

What I don't like is remembering the past. This last client has erased everything I've worked so hard to build, and shattered it like fragile glass with one session. The confident woman that walked into this room, is now a sniveling little girl curled up on her bed waiting for her daddy to punish her again.

"Daddy, no! I'm sorry! I'll be good!" My cheeks never seem to be dry, the snot running down the top of my lips. How long does it take before your eyes dry up forever?

The sexually sadistic lovers I can handle, but the full on sadists for the sake of pain - it fucks with my psyche. I really believed I was beyond it all. Oh how *very* wrong I am.

My father used to come home every night pissed at the world. Nothing we did was good enough for him. He hated everything my mom cooked and continually bitched about it. But it was so much worse if she had nothing ready. That little girl emerges and takes over my mind with a slideshow of my past.

"What the fuck is this? You call this food?" The loud crack of his slap on her face makes me wince as I stand there with my hands clasped together and face tilted down. I don't know what to do when he's like this.

"After everything I do for you two? Fucking worthless! Can't even fucking make a decent meal after the blood, sweat, and tears I have to go through each day?"

"I-I'm sorry. I'll try harder next-" The crack of the slap this time makes me scream and cover my ears. I didn't mean to, it just slipped out.

"And you, I can't even look at you." His foot falls are heavy and ominous, coming toward me.

I'm going to die tonight.

I'm a disgrace because I was born female. A son would have suited him better. He would force me to sit on the floor and be his foot-rest after he finished eating. *For a solid three hours, I would sit on the floor while his feet were on my shoulders.* If I moved, and I always did, since I was only five, he would beat me until I blacked out.

My mother knew better than to defend me, or she would end up with broken appendages. Nothing was ever safe around my dad. He was a ticking time bomb just waiting to explode, taking casualties with him.

I thought I was beyond this. I thought I was numb enough. I thought...

Click.

When the door handle turns, I wake from my nightmarish slumber. At least that's what it feels like. But I've been awake, haven't I? A shadow falls over me and I almost jump off the bed thinking it's my father's face I will see. My arms ache again from the twisted way I had to maneuver myself to find a comfortable position while still tied up to this bed of horrors.

"What happened to you?" The voice is feminine, frantic. And *that* in itself calms me a bit.

It's not him. He's gone. He's been gone.

I killed him.

Not before his debtors came to collect what he used as collateral. *Me.*

My head is still so foggy from my last session that I can't seem to make out who is talking. It's one of the girls. It has to be. *Please. Someone. Anyone!*

I think I'm seeing double, then triple, then beautiful darkness.

∼

NADYA

Seeing Magda lying broken on that bed tears me apart. She is one of the strongest among us, except for Madame. Unsure of what to do, I run out to the hallway and call out to the girls who aren't busy.

"I need help! Someone! Hurry!"

"What happened?" One of the girls comes out of her room with a serious expression despite her state of undress.

"I-it's Magda. She needs help!"

Some of the other girls come running as I rush back over to unlatch Magda's restraints. Who would do such a thing? No one is this brazen to fuck with one of us like this. It's unheard of.

By the time the other girls make it inside, all of us are

looking about the room and trying to gently move our sister on the bed.

She moans and we stop midstep. The tears wetting her face churns my stomach. Memories of a time I want to bury threaten to rise up in my mind.

The other girls are mirroring the same expression I have. If someone as strong as Magda is left like this, who's to say we're not next? *Are we next?* Is this what the House of Eden is becoming? Suspicions and conspiracy theories run through my mind as we look over Magda's battered body.

"Is that?"

Our collective gasps reverberate when we all stare at her leg.

"That can't possibly..."

Holding in my gag, I grit my teeth down and nudge the other girls to keep moving her gently so that the three of us can clean her up. One of the girls is inspecting the wound on Magda's leg, and a small whimper escapes her lips making us all snap our heads in her direction. She tries to be brave and find something to clean it out with. The site is grizzly and one that will be burned into the back of my mind forever. I'm scared, but I'm also pissed.

Where is the Mistress? How can she not know?

"Magda, don't worry. We got you. We're going to fix this." I don't know how much of my whispered encouragement will help, but it's better than nothing.

Quietly, my mind tries to communicate to hers, telling her that we'll avenge her somehow. We have to. This is the House of Eden. We protect our own.

Magda's head lolls to the side and one of the girls caresses her hair back and wipes her tear stained cheeks. How she has stayed awake this long baffles my mind. She is so strong and we cannot lose her. Magda moans on and off again incoherently.

The girls and I continue to wipe the blood and what smells like piss from her body.

Sick men and their debauchery.

One of her moans becomes louder right as Erdene walks in.

My chest feels tight and my face feels hot. I'm not sure whether my anger should be extended toward the Mistress or not. After all, she controls the clientele. We all watch as she walks around the room, taking everything in with a shrewd look on her face.

Twirling her fingers around, she signals for us to vacate the room. What does she not want us to see, or hear, I wonder? I linger, not wanting to leave an injured sister like that. Indecision runs through me, fear of punishment against loyalty. The Mistress gives me a moment before shooting a glare at me.

Fear wins. Obediently, I walk out of Magda's room with retribution on my mind.

MAGDA

My mind is fading in and out. The pain is vacillating between throbbing, unbearable, and numbing me from the inside. In between the small increments of reprieve, I feel hands all over me - soft ones.

Not like Daddy's, not like Mister Spence. Someone touches me again and my mind tries to pull me from the darkness threatening to engulf me once more.

When my eyelids finally stop feeling heavy, I force them open and see Erdene holding my hand. In confusion, I wonder if I've lost myself into another reality, one where she would actually show affection like this.

She sighs loudly and the illusion is broken. The wound is

somewhere between irritating and numbing. Shit, I'd feel like sighing too if my mind isn't so indecisive on how to take the pain that still lingers on my leg.

"I did this to you." Erdene's words are so blunt.

I'm not sure how to take it. The softening of her facial expression only lasts but a second, or maybe I'm seeing things.

"No, *he did*." Let's not play in the realm of denial. It helps none of us.

We all know it's possible for any of our client's to take things too far. We are only whores in their eyes, after all.

Simple flesh suits for the simple pleasures of men.

Except that's not true, is it? Nothing in life is simple.

"I brought him to you." She reiterates with a stubborn look on her face.

Yeah, you sure did, and you purposely gave him to me.

"I will not take him again as a client." Just like that, the problem is solved.

Nothing in life is that simple. Daddy taught me that.

The girls of the House of Eden do not have the luxury to choose our futures here. But I can't help thinking this would be *the incident* that would make me choose to leave the house once and for all. Leave this life of debauchery behind. One thing is for sure, the Mistress will be left in the dust of my exit if I ever see that evil man again.

My eyes must convey my thoughts because Erdene looks at me, affronted. "Do you think so little of me that I would subject any of you to this again?"

Wouldn't she? I should be the one affronted since the jackass was sent to *me*!

Burying my anger into the pit of my tender stomach, I shrug in nonchalance. I sincerely hope not because I won't survive another session like that.

For *me* to admit that took a lot. I'm one of the few girls who has been with Erdene at this house the longest, besides Möngö-maa. We three have seen all the ugly and most depraved souls come and go in this place since our teenage years. It was only after Erdene took hold of this ship, not always through blood-less means, that things started to look up. The House of Eden finally became some sort of semblance of a home.

But if she keeps bringing in clients like him, the house she has worked so hard to build will fall. An empire burned to the ground and forgotten among the destruction we let breach our very home.

Chapter Six

ERDENE

The bastard.

My girls can handle a lot of stuff thrown at them. But this? This is something else. My skin prickles with the need for something, something to dig my claws into. The man didn't even have a fetish for what he was doing, according to what I've gathered.

It was entirely a torture session.

This is exactly why I *had* to go see Alexander Jones earlier today. We need the money to increase our security in the house so issues like this *never* arise again. The house's control needs to remain ours.

Determination courses through me and I remove myself from Magda's room before my volatile emotions lead me to make decisions I may regret. Walking downstairs toward the main lobby, I look for Jessi. She is one of our oldest workers, until I transferred her to the front. One of her last client's, during the old regime, beat her so badly he broke her femur and it never healed right again, causing her to limp when the weather gets bad.

After taking control of the House, I made sure to still give her a safe place to stay by training her in hosting newcomers as well as informing them of our membership program. That way she remains an integral part of our system without having to service the clientele with her body.

Her bitterness toward the old regime helps our current House in her shrewdness when dealing with potential new clientele. She makes sure they follow the rules in order to even be considered on the list.

But of course, you get the snakes that make it into our garden under the pretense of something else, like Mister Spence.

"Jessi, do you have a second?"

She looks up from the computer and paperwork currently in front of her and nods.

"Of course, Mistress. What do you need?"

"Check the accounts and let me know if a sizable amount has been deposited."

"Yes, Mistress." Without question, her fingers work quickly, the sounds of clicks going faster and faster. Our system isn't the greatest, but it's done us well up to this point.

"There has been a deposit, yes."

"Good. I'm going to task you with a specific job. Gather a couple of the girls and get started on increasing our security and upgrading our computers. I trust you'll know what to do, Jessi. We can't have our sisters brought down with the old ship - with the way things used to be. We need to be better. We need to reign over our territory and bring the clientele to *their* knees, not the other way around."

"I understand, Mistress. You can trust me."

"Take Magda off the list. She needs to recover from her last client. Have her down here with you to help with the decision making. Report to me in a week on your progress."

"Yes, Mistress."

Nodding my head, I turn on my heel and walk toward my back office. Once inside, I plant myself on the seat behind the small desk. The room is not as opulent as Alexander's, but one thing at a time.

Rubbing my hand down my face, I think of Magda. I'm going to need to call in a doctor to look at her leg. I can't let the wound fester until infection sets in, creating an even bigger breeding ground for other complications.

The House of Eden used to have an in-house doctor. But he was part of the old regime. I didn't want him to continue with us. The only problem now is, I have a hard time trusting new people as well.

What to do, what to do.

Sitting up straight in the chair, I move it as close to the desk as I can get before turning on the computer. The database Jessi works on is also linked here, but the speed of the network and connection is atrocious. How the men used to manage the place with this stuff is beyond me.

Once the clientele files finally come up on the screen, I start scouring through the extensive list. From current members, members on temporary probation, and members on the waiting list, I start comparing them on a separate window to find out as much as I can about each person I'm considering.

My time at the House of Eden hasn't afforded the education I probably need for this, but my skills with debauchery *have* afforded me enough of a glimpse, through the men who felt sorry for me, for what I need to run a brothel.

There.

My eyes stop on one person in particular. Michael Scott, age thirty six. Has been a member of the House of Eden for five years. No complaints from any of the girls. I think I remember something about him, something one of the girls said about his skill with his hands. Staring at his face, I memorize his features so I don't miss him the next time he comes in.

Typing a message to Jessi via the computer, I ask her to bring down all the girls who have been with Mister Scott, member number 6439A. She responds quickly, and I minimize my window before leaving the office. My heels click toward the lobby where I find Nadya and Isla standing in waiting.

"Nadya, Isla. You've taken Mister Michael Scott, yes? Stands about six foot two, average build, blond hair, blue eyes." I address my girls casually.

"Yes, Mistress. He's one of my regulars." My eyes turn to Nadya at her response.

"I had him a few times in the beginning. When Nadya is booked with appointments, he occasionally comes to my room."

So Nadya is his favorite with Isla as second. "Nadya, were you the one who mentioned something about his hands?"

"His hands, Mistress?"

"What do you know about him? What does he do for a living?"

"Oh, I see. Yes, it's something to do with his hands. I remember him mentioning something about precision every time he touches me and takes off my clothes."

Turning to Isla, I lift an eyebrow to ask her the same question mentally.

"Oh, um. I don't remember much since we don't do much talking when he enters my room. But I think I remember him mentioning something about keeping cuts straight."

I think I'm going to have to get to the point in order to get the answers I'm looking for. "We need a new house doctor. Doctor Gram Hudson will no longer continue to provide us medical services since his membership has become void. Nadya, Isla. Whoever Mister Michael Scott chooses to visit, make sure you find out what he does for a living. If my assumptions are correct, convince him by *whatever means necessary* to come on board."

"Yes, Mistress." The girl's echo each other in unison.

Waving my hand to dismiss them, I turn to Jessi. "Has Magda come down to help you yet?"

"Not yet, Mistress. One of the girls is still tending to her wound and said she will help her downstairs soon."

"Okay, good. Keep me updated on her status."

"Yes, Mistress."

Heading back to the office, I sit down at the desk and bring up the membership window again. Scrolling with my right hand on the mouse, I start to type a name into the search bar and hit enter. The bastard's face comes up and my fingers quickly change the status of member 3957A from active to terminated. Mister Spence won't miss the full cost of his yearly membership as the contract states clients can be terminated at any time if the rules and policies are not followed.

Nowhere in our damn clause does it allow a man to start eating the flesh of my girls. No, Mister Spence is going to have to find his meals and pussy somewhere else in the city.

Chapter Seven

MAGDA

Being treated as a victim is not who I am. I don't want anyone's pity. We all came from something in the House of Eden. I'm no different. It's going to be a while before I can take on any more customers. However, there are other duties I can complete.

Here in the pits of the house, we have extracurricular activities in the basement. That is what made Erdene such a perceptive and canny businesswoman. If you fuck with her, you end up in her basement of horrors. Mistress Erdene can suck your dick one moment, then slice your throat the next and I admire her for it.

In the current mood I'm in, I really need time in the basement to do something, *anything*.

"Good for nothing cunt! Why do you keep putting yourself in these situations, huh? It could have been so simple if you would have just done what I said! But no, instead now we're here. Don't look at me like that when you know you brought it on yourself."

"I'm sorry, Daddy."

I'm more angry with myself than Mr. Spence. At the end of the day, I *allowed* myself to be his casualty. He took what he wanted simply because I allowed it. Now, he literally had a pound of my flesh - inside of him. I should have done something. I should have reacted better, protected myself. Dammit!

I've been summoned to Erdene's office but I can't deal with that right now. I need to clear my head. Find that peaceful state. The Mistress can punish me if she wants. After Helga assists me with my wounds, I can't take the pity in her eyes anymore.

I lose it.

I yell at her when I shouldn't be, projecting all my frustrations of the situation and the old memories shrouding my mind in darkness and anger. Grinding my teeth inside my mouth to prevent myself from growling at the other girls, I wordlessly leave my quarters.

What a sight I must be to everyone in the hallway witnessing it all. Unbreakable Magda, limping and hobbling all the way down to the basement.

Fuck this! Fuck all these men and their stupid appetites for the destruction of women!

Going for the punching bag located on the other side of the basement, my fists land on it hard, shaking the chain it's hanging on. The previous men in charge used this space in their down time, some of the other rooms were used to conduct shady business. Thanks to Erdene, now it belongs to all us girls.

Memories of Mister Spence and my father start at the forefront of my mind the moment the heavy bag swings back from my hit. My hands are already in fists before it even makes it close enough to me to throw the second punch. The chain jingles and rattles with the impact.

Damn these men, damn them all to hell. Damn myself for

letting it get that far and letting myself fall victim to another man's rage. I thought I was beyond that now, after all these years.

I thought I've shoved that pathetic little girl so deep inside of myself she would have no way out.

Throwing some uppercuts and jabs, my body moves on its own accord, trying to expend the anger within me. Only after the initial throb of my knuckles do I realize that I didn't even bother to wrap my hands. The smell of cold concrete and disinfected metal is harsh in my nostrils, burning the hairs the harder I breathe. I want to feel the pain of every hit, imagine his face - both of their faces - as I continue to throw punch after punch. My knuckles are going to pay the price later. The sting of the open wounds upon impact makes me bare my teeth in rage.

Mister Spence dredged up the memories I worked so hard to squash down about my childhood. I was so good at keeping my emotions in check, then *one* man comes in and unravels it all.

It fucking pisses me off.

My shoulders are starting to feel tired and sore, not being used for so long in this way before, and with such intensity. The reverberation of each hit, vibrates through my very bones.

Left, right, left, right.

I could kill him. I could kill him right now if he was here.

The sneer on Mister Spence's face morphs into my father's and my eyes see red, or maybe it's the blood that's starting to coat the outside of the heavy bag. Feeling a hand on my shoulder, I automatically swing around, thankful that Erdene is smart enough to bob and weave so my fist doesn't connect with her face. She sends me a glare, but can't hold the stare when she notices the state I'm in.

"I have a contract that was fulfilled. You want it?" The tone of her voice is impassive, but there's a spark in her eyes that blinks out within a second.

The Mistress is the master of her emotions. I need to channel her strength right now.

I simply nod in response, my mental state exhausted from what I unleashed on the heavy bag. The Mistress is hard on us, but she's also good to us. Contracts in the House of Eden are a treat for the girls who need to take out their frustrations. Our extracurricular activities are kept between the sisters, a secrecy we take to our deathbed.

The sound of the team strapping the unlucky soul down on the table drifts to my ears from the adjacent room. Their footsteps and shuffles echo around us as well as the sounds of a struggle.

The original shady business brought in by the old regime is something Erdene held onto as an extra source of income for the House. There is an underground network of hits put out on individuals for whatever reason it may be - the reason is not our problem.

Money talks and money has power. Men aren't the only ones who are capable of fulfilling these contracts.

"Mmmmph!"

Slap!

"Mmmph!"

"Would you just shut up already? Geez."

"This guy doesn't give up."

When Erdene's hunters procure an individual, she collects the money. We do our thing here and then send proof of death. One lucky sister gets to take her anger out on the hit. The only time she's ever made all of her girls watch is when someone betrays her and she needs to make a point.

Cici knew that.

Once the muffled voices stop and the two girls leave, Erdene and I head to the other room. There, lying on the metal table near our supplies is an average sized male with dark hair and equally dark eyes. He scowls when I walk in his periphery even though it won't do him any good. The ladies at the House of Eden are used to smiles, scowls, and everything in between. From men who worship us on their knees to the ones that force us on our knees for their pleasure.

"Mmmph! Mmmmph!"

He's trying to articulate something but the gag in his mouth muffles it, his words coming out incomprehensible. *How does it feel, hmm?* Why do they always feel the need to try? I have no desire to hear what hate he wants to spew, so I leave the material in.

Didn't you do the same? Grinding my teeth down, I try to tamp down the memory I only just subdued earlier.

The light metal clanging is the only thing that can be heard above the man's continuous muffled noises. The light taps of Erdene's heels tell me she's already on her way back up into the main part of the house. Before she makes it past the first few steps, she gives me a final look over her shoulder. Stopping my preparation, I give her my full attention. Her expression is something I can't decipher and don't care to.

Once I bring my attention back to the task, the sound of Erdene's heels *click click* up the stairs. She's just going to have to forgive me for dismissing her with my eyes. She knows better than to bother me when I'm in the zone like this - when my need for something physical is so high. My eyes scan everything available in front of me. Grabbing a hunting knife off of the magnetic holder, I bring it over to the bound man. His initial expression never wavers and I wonder if he's been in this position before. He has no fear. Maybe he does not sense the gravity of the situation. After all, what could possibly happen in a brothel - a house of whores?

Pulling out the contract, I read it to him. He needs to understand that he is here for a death sentence. That he needs to savor the moments of his last breath while he can. About halfway through my speech, his mind finally comprehends that he is at his eleventh hour, his eyes widen in a comical way. I know my small stature surprises many who end up down here. How can a tiny whore be capable of the brutal, savage things I do? It's an advantage I don't take lightly.

"Mr. Favre. You are set to be executed today by any means I see necessary. This contract was taken out by your father-in-law, a Mister Grober." My eyes flick to his and watch as he stares at me in anger. Not a surprise then. Keeping it in the family. "He claims you are the reason his daughter is not able to conceive an heir, and he wishes for her to remarry."

Death by shooting blanks.

The man looks at me like I've lost my mind. Hey, I'm not the one who put a hit on him. I'm still pissed from earlier and maybe I do come off as 'off kilter'. It's only thanks to men like him. I'm still riding the high of my previous heavy bag session; the anger not yet dissipated out of my system despite the continuous throbbing in my knuckles.

I don't care why he's here. It's not my problem. He reminds me of my father in some ways and that alone pisses me off. *Men, men, men.* I'm basically a higher class whore now, from where I've once started, but it doesn't stop the old emotions overflowing out of me. Does one ever heal completely from these things? The memories get dredged up when they're uninvited, making the scars become scabs again. Grabbing the knife, the glint of the steel against his face makes his eyes widen once more, sending a thrill up my spine. Control is a heady thing around these parts. The muffled screams barely register as I carve my initials into his skin - as per the request of the buyer.

"Mmmphhh!!" His pathetic attempts continue to go unnoticed.

I'm softly laughing as he struggles against his restraints. Such a lively one. The crimson bloom on his flesh makes me crave more. With the knife still dripping with blood, I toss it onto the tray nearby with a loud clatter and look around. *Hmm, what next?* My eyes land on something that makes me smile. Taking a pair of pliers this time, I remove his finger nails one by one.

"Ahhh!" I scream at the top of my lungs with him like a duet.

Does that make me naughty? Does it make it sound crazy? *Fuck it.* I need this contract. Need this connection. The Mistress knew it. I need to release the frustration Mister Spence built up within me and sometimes just screaming for no damn reason *fucking* helps.

Tears drip down his face as he moans in pain after the last nail is removed. I really thought he would last longer than this. How disappointing I mean, I wish *I* could have just been left alone to moan in pain too. *But he never left me alone, did he? He never gave me a fucking break, not for one second of the day.* Dropping the pliers on the ground with a loud *thud,* the sound of metal on concrete bounces off the walls reminding the man of how alone we truly are down here.

It's just a party for two tonight.

Taking the small ax off of the wall, I twist my wrist testing the weight and balance before I swing it down with all my might to chop off his wrist. The sound of the snap lets me know just how sharp the weapons are kept down here. The girls do a wonderful job at upkeep. Feeling giddy, I tell myself his fingers have to be easier.

Swish! Snap!

Snap!

Snap!

Each one comes off with one solid swing of the ax.

Snap. Snap.

Each one falling to the ground, leaving a small trail of blood along their path. My eyes watch with morbid fascination, the fury I felt before finally simmers down enough for me to start to feel pleasure again.

I realize he's not moving. This isn't going to do. This isn't becoming a party of one just yet. How rude can this asshole be? He needs to wake up and keep me company down here.

He always woke me up when I tried to escape in my mind, in my sleep. He beat me daily as a child. He needed to pay for it. My father was horrendous. Daddy has to pay for the way his fingers always roamed where they shouldn't have, the way his eyes used to track me when he didn't think I noticed because I always had my head down.

Taking my thumbs, I put one in each eye and push as hard as I can. The pressure against the pads of my fingers is a feeling that brings up other memories. Why is his asshole doing this to me? He's supposed to help ease my mind, not make it more tumultuous! My fingers keep pushing harder and harder until his eyes both pop like squishy grapes, the fluids exploding over the top of my thumbs. Ugh, and, of course, the bastard's not going to be the one to help me clean up this mess. *Typical.*

"Ahhhh!" At least the eye gouging wakes him up, sending a new bout of muffled screams to fill the basement once more.

"Welcome back, sleeping beauty." *Now we can really play.* Smiling as I back up toward the tray, my hands reach for the familiar handle.

His head is lolling side to side, his moans coming out as soft groans like a lover who has just climaxed inside a hot, wet pussy. *Naughty man.* I haven't reached my climax yet. He should know better. In a frenzy, I stab him over and over. Left, right.

Up, down, up, down. The warmth of the spray on my face makes me moan as my tongue licks up the copper taste, my eyes never wavering from his sitting figure.

In this short relationship, it's only fair we both get our pleasure out of this rendezvous. His head falls back like a man in the throws of ecstasy. *No one said he was allowed to cum just yet.* Not before I've had my fill. I can feel the smile on my face twist into a snarl as my hands continue to come down again and again. *Selfish, selfish man. They're all so selfish!* Running out of room to play, my sights zone in on his pristine neck, and I jerk my arm in a wide arc, watching the crimson line bloom and spurt like a fountain.

Beautiful. Macabre.

I don't remember limping back up the stairs. I don't really remember showering and lying down on the bed in my quarters. None of the girls came by to check up on me, though the sounds of their footsteps come and go like the static on my mother's old TV. The sound of light moans and groans from the other side of the walls is a sore reminder that I'm still home at the House of Eden. Or maybe I'm back home with my father with the sound of porno playing in the background as my mother's muffled screams escape every now and again from behind my father's hand, suffocating her as he fucks her.

I bet Mister Favre came more times than I did while he sat on that chair in the basement. Every time the knife came down, my heart sped up. The same way it does when I fuck a client into oblivion. I'm pretty sure Erdene came by not long ago while I'm lost in this slow descent to madness.

"Was it really necessary to stab the poor man eighty-seven times." Is she speaking to me or am I dreaming?

Was it necessary? Every time I looked at him, my eyes changed who I saw. One moment it would be my father's face, the next it would be Mister Spence.

Memories of the past few hours come back in pieces as my eyes become heavier the longer I lay on this bed.

The bed was clean and made when I entered. So, it's not just my imagination, the Mistress really is on my side.

My fugues have not happened like this since I left my father's house. Erdene and I have been through a lot together. And now, she's finally seen me at my lowest.

Chapter Eight

ERDENE

Jessi is able to complete her task with the help of the other girls within a week's time. Mister Spence tried to appeal his membership, but has since been banned from the premises. The time for upgraded security is now crucial in case of retaliation.

Walking out of my office, I look around. We've haven't had this amount of men standing in the lobby since the old regime, when the higher ups were throwing girls around like candy prizes for undocumented jobs gone well.

"Men. I'm sure you all know why you're here."

"Aye. You the lady in charge?"

Ignoring his question, I continue to pace in front of the small crowd. The girls are standing toward the back by the front lobby desk and computer. The men, they haven't taken their eyes off me yet, some with their sights straying to particular body parts. When it comes time to get the job done, I hope these men have better attention spans than what most of them are showing me now.

"Gentlemen. I need you to understand that insubordination will *not* be tolerated. You may be tempted to take a taste of the flesh we have here, but make no mistake, my girls know I run a tight ship. Is this clear?"

Some snickers escape.

"What exactly do you need from us?" My eyes shoot to the red-headed man who voices this question.

"Jessi should have informed you of our operations here. The ladies of the house are *gold*, our most precious commodity. Cameras will soon be set up in specific locations in order to make sure our clients are following the rules. Men, you will be tasked to remove *anyone* who feels like they're above the House of Eden. I do not care *how* they are removed, I just ask that they be removed *permanently* without any repercussions that come back on us. Whatever it takes, but keep the House *untouchable*."

"What if we get an offer from one of the ladies?"

I stop my pacing and turn to look at the gruffest looking male here. With his five 'o clock shadow, a scar bisecting his left eye leaving it cloudy, and cocky grin, I can already tell this one will be a handful.

"Why, pray tell, would any of *my* ladies do that?"

The men collectively laugh as I quietly wait for his answer.

"Because they might see me around and want a little taste." He licks his lips in emphasis but I'm not phased. We've had plenty of men like him around the House as well as in our basement.

"My ladies know *who* they should and shouldn't open their legs for." Though I do hope he tries. He might get more than he can chew with my girls. They all play the role of dainty maidens well. Turning away from him, I point my gaze at Jessi. "Hand me the roster you've created."

"Yes, Mistress."

Masculine whispers of 'Mistress' float behind my back but I ignore it, keeping my posture unaffected.

Jessi quickly comes to my side with papers that are stapled neatly. Looking it over, I see she has ranked them in regards to their years of experience in their line of work.

"Mister Reeves." Lifting my head, I turn to scan the room until I see a specific male stand at attention. He's older, more battle worn and looks to have a permanent scowl on his face. *Good*. "You will be placed in the supervisory role among these men. I trust this isn't your first rodeo?"

"Not really, but it's my first in such an... establishment." His voice is steady and sure. His gaze is a laser point. I'm liking his dominating aura already. He should be able to keep these men in line.

"The work's the same. Think of the ladies here as our products. You understand?"

"Yes... *Mistress*. I understand just fine."

He catches on quickly, I see.

Turning my gaze to the others, I make sure to make my voice stern. "Money will be sent at the end of each month to your accounts. Anyone who still chooses to stay on, please see Mister Reeves. Anyone who wants to change their mind, leave my House. *Now*. That will be all, gentlemen."

Turning on my heel, I walk myself toward the back office without another glance back. What needs to be said has been said. Hopefully these boys know how to follow the rules laid down.

Jessi is also tasked to upgrade our networking system and she's done her job well. A new computer sits on my desk as well as new cameras in a box on the floor. Bending over to look at the equipment, a masculine voice clears behind me.

"Um... Mistress, was it? I uh..."

Looking over my shoulder without straightening up, I catch

Mister Reeves staring right at my ass in the pencil skirt I chose to wear today.

"Yes, Mister Reeves?"

He clears his throat again before swallowing. "Yes, well, I've got the boys all sorted out. Just wanted to check in and see if there is anything else I can help you with."

The previous scowl that was on his face earlier has subtly morphed into something else.

"How chivalrous of you." Straightening up, I turn to him fully. "It would be nice to have someone set up these cameras around the place."

"Yeah, I got a guy that goes way back. He's good with that kind of shit. I'll hit him up."

Connections, I see. So he says.

"If you vouch for him, Mister Reeves, know that anything that happens lands on your shoulders as well."

"I got you. I trust him."

Trust is a mercurial word.

Turning to wave my hand toward the box, I give him a smirk. "Have at it then. Let me know when you finish. I would like for all the cameras to be directed into a specific computer."

"I assume it will be mine."

"You assume correctly for the most part, but I will also have access as well."

A little smirk appears on his face, softening his features. "Got it. I'll get my guy on it."

"See that you do."

Watching him move around the room, bend his knees and pick up the box, my eyes become fixated on the way the muscles play under his shirt.

With his hands full, his permanent scowl softens as he responds. "Yes, Mistress."

With heavy booted steps, he exits my office and I bring

myself behind my desk to turn on my new computer. Bringing up Michael Scott's account, I look him over again under his new file as the House Doctor. The girls did well to persuade him to come on board. He enjoyed every minute of their attention together. Another satisfied customer.

Next on the agenda, picking up more contracts for my girls to keep their skills up.

Chapter Nine

As I leave the establishment, I know the guys are going to razz me about going into the Mistress' office. I recognize a few of them from some side jobs I've done in the past.

They can laugh all they want, but the fact is, the money is good. What the Mistress of the house is offering is better than I've ever made. Money aside, this job sounds like it's going to be steady and it's a way for me to make up for letting my daughter slip away. Trying not to think of the past, my mind focuses on everything that needs to be done and what the House of Eden needs in terms of security.

By the looks of it, this place has never had any type of security set up. How these ladies remained unharmed up to this point is beyond me. A house full of whores? Sounds like the perfect setup for a human trafficking ring. But things happen for a reason, and something brought me here today besides the connection that called me out of the blue.

Maybe this is my second chance - a chance to make things right by guarding these young women. Maybe I could inadvertently be saving someone else's daughter. *The way I couldn't save mine.*

The guilt that weighs me down is not as heavy today. Not after solidifying my position with the House.

Heading over to Jinder's, I want to make sure he is available for the camera setup. He and I go way back - back during my darker days. It doesn't change the fact that he's brilliant at what he does. Pulling up in front of his home, a man with an air of authority leaves his front door but not before shaking Jinder's hand. I hope I'm not too late to snag him. Underground jobs come in all fashions. Watching until the gentleman gets into the driver's side of his vehicle, I wait until the engine starts before getting out of my own vehicle.

The light sound of the tires going over gravel cracks behind me as I walk up to Jinder's front door. He must have noticed my arrival because he waves me in before I even reach his single front step.

"Hey stranger." When is the last time I came by?

Shaking his proffered hand, I pull him in for a hug, patting him on his back. He had been a good friend when my daughter was missing and that's something I will never forget. Jinder had really been there for me when I couldn't even be there for myself.

"To what do I owe this visit?" He asks in his thick accent, and gestures at a padded chair.

Smiling, I sit down and get right into the reason for my arrival. "I landed a stable gig."

"Yeah?"

"Yeah. It's not in the most savory of places, but that's nothing new." I shrug.

"So, what makes it more stable than any of our other jobs?"

Leaning back in the chair, I get comfortable. I haven't been back here in a while, but everything still looks the same.

"The lady that runs the joint wants me as head of her security."

He nods. "What happened to her last one?"

"She never had one."

The statement makes Jinder stare at me for a moment. He correctly makes his assumptions with his next question. "How is that possible with a house full of women?"

"Beats me. But a couple of the guys we ran into on the last few jobs were there too."

Jinder, with his elbows on his knees, leans back and laces his fingers behind his head. His eyes remain sharp despite the smirk plastered on his face.

"I thought you didn't want to work with those asshats anymore? I remember a few of them not playing well with others."

"Yeah, well. I'm sure this will be no different. In a house full of that much pussy, there's bound to be a dick swinging contest. For now, they're all under my command which leads me to why I'm here today."

"What do you need me to do? Actually, before we get to business, where is this house of ill repute you speak of?" My eyes narrow at his question.

"Why do you need to know? What difference does it make?"

"Relax, Reeves. I'm just curious."

The asshole is nosey is what he is - and that's exactly why he's good at what he does. If I don't tell him now, he'll just find out later on his own, anyway. Might as well shave off some time.

"The House of Eden."

"The whore house that's three towns over? I thought it was run by some sleaze." He stares at me for a few seconds. "Honestly, I'm surprised, my friend, that you would frequent such an establishment."

Ignoring the jab, I give him a glare. "You know I've only just come back to town. I don't know what the history of this place is and, honestly, I don't really care. My job is to set up the shit that needs to be set up and protect the commodities inside."

"Pfft." Despite his stupid response, Jinder nods before getting up to walk toward the back of his house where his equipment is set up. Following him, I watch as he punches a code in to unlock the door.

Finally deciding to answer the last statement, I clear my throat and give him a serious look. "I don't use the House as a patron. However, one of the young female employees was recently assaulted."

His look says it all. *That's the profession she is in.* Walking over to his chair, he motions me to sit down in one beside him.

"Not sexually, physically." Her limp made me take notice. But it was the inquiry I made with the front desk girl that gave me what I needed to know. "This man was extremely brutal, to the point of eating her flesh," I pause to shake the mental image from my mind. "Look, I came to the establishment to see what the job was about and ended up heading up the new security team. Seems these ladies need someone like me to make sure that this type of behavior never happens again."

He looks at me thoughtfully. He knew women who were being abused. Especially after the way we recovered my daughter, Celia's body, it became a hard issue with both of us. Going after the ones who did just wasn't enough. It will never be enough. It will never bring her back.

The sound of Jinder's voice breaks me out of my dark memories. "I just signed up on another contract, but what you're asking shouldn't take me long. I'm assuming they need a security system set up and for the program to be loaded into the mainframe, correct?" His fingers fly across the keyboard, bringing up the location on the map. "Oddly enough, your job and mine aren't far from each other." He stops there, and I know not to press him about his business. I am just happy to get him to help me with this.

"Take this number down. In case the lady running the place and signing my checks has any questions about anything and wants to hear it from the source."

"No need. I already got it."

"Of course."

A few moments of silence goes by with only the sound of a keyboard.

"Alright, there ya go. I hacked into the current computers in the establishment and uploaded the software for ya."

Hopefully, the Mistress doesn't notice it before I get back.

"Thanks, man. As always."

"Sure, sure."

By the time I leave his front door, the sun is already setting beyond the horizon. Going home that night, I know the dreams will invade me again. Especially after hearing what happened to that girl with the limp. Moving around the house, going through the motions, my mind wanders to the past despite telling it not to. I was sober when we found her, but damn these memories. It is so hard not to run out and buy a bottle of whiskey to feel the burn sliding down my throat, making me forget all the shit I allowed to happen because I was drunk off my ass and not being a father. Wrong place, wrong time, wrong choices.

Downing a glass of water, I pretend it's the alcohol I wish it to be. When I get to the bedroom of my apartment, I fall face first into the mattress.

What the hell am I doing taking jobs at this age anyway? It's these stupid jobs that drive me to drink - and it's because of these stupid jobs that I wasn't there in time.

The memories of trying to off myself when they found the

remnants of her body hit me like a sledgehammer. The emotions of drowning in darkness, consuming the vision around me. Feels like only yesterday and far away all at the same time. Jinder is the one who found me hanging from the rafters. If he would've gotten there five minutes later - hell two minutes later - I would be six feet under.

At least I would be with her.

The soul shattering pain was too much to bear, but Jinder made me face it. He took me to therapy daily. He forced my ass off my couch and dragged me into the damn shower where he proceeded to turn the cold water on over my head to shake me out of shit.

The memory of Jinder's voice over the sound of water, plays back in my head.

"It's not your fucking fault, man. Get that through your thick skull!"

I still could have been a better father. Groaning, I turn and lie on my side, willing myself to sleep off these thoughts. I could have taken notice of the monster running around defiling girls, but instead, my head was too wrapped up in the massacre we had come across on the previous job. I drowned myself in alcohol trying to will away one image, only to get another to take its place.

Growling, I slap the side of my head to try and shake this shit off. The authorities never caught him. I never caught him. But I caught every slimeball that was connected to him and found out every little detail I could. Visions of red cloud the back of my eyelids. I will never stop looking for him. If taking this position helps at least one person sleep better at night, then I've done my job.

I failed Celia. I refuse to fail anyone else.

Chapter Ten

ERDENE

"Good morning." I greet my new head of security.

"Good morning. I wanted to show you what we completed overnight."

Without looking at him, my heels click toward the front lobby area. Jessi gives me a nod in greeting and I smile at her in return. Opening the office door, a cool draft wafts our way, letting me know it stayed nice and unoccupied while I was away. Many nights are spent sleeping in the adjacent room but sometimes there's business to be had in other places.

Places being Mister Alexander Jones' backseat with my skirt pushed up to my waist. It was the same speech when we finished.

"I hope to never see you again." Whatever you say, Mister Jones. Whatever you say.

My pussy clenches at the memory while my fingers turn the computer on. Bending over my desk, I stare at the login screen. The cameras work perfectly. Mister Reeves' connection really outdid himself. Not only do the cameras record the perfect angles, there's also an infrared option. The simple fact that all of this was set up and the room feels like no one had entered earlier comes up as a mental flag. Curiosity has me wondering about Mister Reeves' past but the logical mind in me says to leave well enough alone. He hasn't broken my trust in any way at this point, instead proving himself again and again with his competence. After all, if any of the girls were messed with, I'm sure it would have been dealt with swiftly - by one of my ladies.

Coming into the house today, the men were all strategically placed in the appropriate locations as far as I can see. They don't overcrowd the front, making our patrons nervous at their presence. It's just the way I like it. Subtle, like predators hidden in the crevices of every corner, hiding behind the jewels of the house.

Straightening, I turn around to find Mister Reeves' arms crossed with a serious look on his face. Is he expecting bad news and for me to spew curses? How very curious.

"Thank you, Mister Reeves. Seems I hired just the right man for the job. Have your men rotate their shifts halfway through the night. Lunch hours will be up to your supervision and decision on how you want to handle it. I only ask that there always be at least a few men on the grounds at all times, even during shift changes."

"You got it."

My lips twitch and I have to force myself not to smile at his oh so grave demeanor. Taking off my jacket slowly, I turn and place it on the back of my office chair. My head peeks over my shoulder to find Mister Reeves looking at my legs. *There it is. Just a man after all.*

Walking seductively toward my office door, I stand there with my own arms crossed over each other and an eyebrow raised. "Unless you have anything else to report to me, I believe that will be all Mister Reeves."

He smirks as he begins to walk toward me.

"Cornell."

Smiling in response to his answer, I give him a once over. You never know what kind of leverage you need working around here. "Cornell."

"See you around, Mistress."

He turns to exit but not before I whisper under my breath, "Erdene." The precious flower that has slowly withered, but somehow survived the life of a female in a world dominated by men who would eat you alive.

Once Mister Reeves is out of sight, I look toward Jessi's desk. She's looking right behind the path our new head of security is taking. She understands that we need to keep our guard up, no matter who says they are on our side.

Slowly blinking, I turn around and head to the back room, but not before I turn the monitor off. The girls are usually good with handling things on their own, and now with the extra men we have watching out for them, I can let out a breath of relief. The blood has since been cleaned off the sheets and floor. The girls are not only good at what they do in the sheets, they're good at taking care of their own.

Walking toward the crate near the closet, I inhale deeply; the smell of chlorine is the only thing burning my nostrils. Flashes of metal bars and the smell of feces hit me like a physical thing even though I know it's only in my mind. I can never prepare for when it comes. It's so sporadic and sometimes it hits me hard, like it is now.

My chest is tight. The woosh of my blood pounds in my ears like I'm back there.

"Get up, whore!"

Thwack! Thwack!

"The worst purchase I've ever had! Look at you! Who the hell wants to fuck skin and bones? How the hell is anyone supposed to

find pleasure between these legs of yours? Good for nothing leech!"

Thwack!

"Ahhh!" The whip comes down right over a badly opened wound and the sting is so sharp, I can feel it to the marrow of my bones - like a lightning bolt through the entirety of my body.

Shaking my head, I groan as I try to dislodge the memory that feels so real. The smell burns in my nose, my gag reflex making me dry heave as I lean against the dog cage.

Slapping against it, my hands suddenly grip the outside of it, shaking the bars to break free.

Get me out! Get me out!

Screaming against closed lips, my eyes burn with frustration at the situation my mind has trapped me in.

My stomach aches, the echo of my starvation at the hands of the man who bought me. You eat and you get punished. You stop eating and you get punished. If you are too fat you get punished. Too thin and you're whipped until death becomes a gift you long for.

My breath stutters as the memory finally fades from my mind's eye. My knees buckle to the ground hard. Sadly, it's the memory of my time with Mister Jones that pulls me from my panic. The hate he spews at me only results in his own loss of control. Each thrust, a chase to make me lose *my* control, a need he has to fulfill despite the words that come out of his mouth. The fact that his vanilla wife is kept safely at home makes me bare my teeth with rage, riding him harder, scratching his chest to leave my mark.

I am Erdene, Mistress of the House of Eden. I will bow to no man. Not anymore.

Chapter Eleven

ERDENE

"**G**irls. This is the last round of customers for the night." I inform them.

They all look at me with questions in their eyes. I've never made this announcement before, but it's important and needs to be done now.

All the ladies turn and go back to their respective rooms.

"Mister Reeves, with me. Jessi, make sure no other patrons come through after the next five guests."

"Yes, Mistress."

"Magda." I need to make sure we keep an eye on her so that infection doesn't set into her wounds. That would be bad for business, we cannot afford to lose any of the girls, not now.

I can see Magda slightly limping and following us in my periphery as I continue to march into my office.

"Shut the door."

Mister Reeves complies and Magda walks to take a seat in front of my desk.

"I'm going to assign one of the men with you from this point forward."

Magda gets up quickly and almost falls over the desk in her objection. I stare down at her, waiting for her to make her decision. My room is so close by, the torture devices I have would change her mind quickly if necessary.

"I can take care of myself."

"Can you?" Glancing at her leg again, I ignore her and turn my gaze toward Mister Reeves. "Spare me one of your men. Have them on her at all times."

"Is there something I need to know?"

"All you need to know is that I might have some... competition coming after me."

"Then why do you need someone on *me*?"

Snapping my head to her, I wonder if she could be this naive in the game of business. "You do realize the easiest way to take down the House is to go after my girls. You are my weak link at this point. One topples and the rest will easily follow."

"Mister Reeves, increase surveillance around the outside of the grounds. We're going to need a couple of men to man the lobby and screen any new patrons that may want to sign up."

"You got it."

Mister Reeves is already mumbling into the radio clipped on his collar as I turn my eyes back to Magda. Hers is blazing right back, but things need to be done in order to secure our place among the male business owners in the same industry.

That picture sent to Mrs. Jones cellphone was a move I *had* to make. Alexander would have never shucked out any more cash and his constant rendezvous with me only served useful for this exact moment.

We take out the competition now, while we still have the element of surprise.

"Erdene! Look at me." I do. "I do not need a guard on me. I can handle myself. *You know this.*"

Flashes of the basement come to mind, but also flashes of her broken on the floor of her room.

"You're a weakness right now. We need to secure any avenues the other houses might use against us. This is why new patrons are to be screened by both Jessi and the men behind her."

Magda stands up and points her finger at me. Her eyes speak of vengeance for my move. I'll take her vengeance. Things must be done. I haven't lasted this long and risen to the top by not calculating my moves.

"You're making a bad decision."

"Am I? Tell me Magda, was it not you who was lying in your room broken and basically eaten?" I lift my lip at the image. She should have fought harder. I taught my girls better than that.

"Just send me where I need to go. I can handle our problems like we always do. Easy as that."

Turning toward her completely, I stare at her hard. Mister Reeves has walked toward the front of the room, hanging out in a dark corner as he watches everything unfold before him.

"Easy. As. That. *You* of all people should know how *not* easy it has been for us! We had to fight and claw our way to survival in this damn house. We had to fight the pack until we dominated and ruled. Do *not* tell me that my moves are done without calculation because I assure you, Magda, if I wanted you to waste your talents away I would have killed you myself to get rid of the problem."

A sharp inhale escapes her but she keeps her face stoic. There's a storm behind her eyes and I know exactly what memories are running through it. I need to make her see the reason for this. Sometimes the only way to ground someone to reality is to dig into the wounds and reopen them.

"You don't mean that. After all we've been through."

"Mister Reeves, go to my room and grab the item in the top left drawer, on the opposite side of my bed."

He nods and silently makes his way past us.

Magda and I are at a standstill. This is the curse of leadership. Decisions are never easy but each decision can put a life at risk. In a house full of females, we would easily be taken into slavery if we weren't keeping ourselves ready for an attack from outside sources. With all the patrons that come through, who are we to say none of them were sent to infiltrate us?

Mister Reeves comes back and hands me my item. I flick my head for him to back up and quickly grab Magda's neck and slam her head down on the desk. She almost tumbles to the ground with her loss of balance. That leg of hers hasn't been healing as fast as it should and she knows it.

Slamming the strap-on onto the table, my hands rip down her pants, my nails inadvertently leaving welts behind on her skin in the process.

"Mister Reeves, would you do me the honor of dressing me?"

The sound of a masculine choke ends quickly as he comes forward and buckles the large dildo onto my front from behind. I can feel his cock becoming semi erect the longer he's behind me.

Magda struggles but I force my forearm behind the back of her neck while gripping her hair and pulling it almost out of her scalp. She hisses and my breasts begin to feel heavy behind the fabrics I wear.

"You're just a little whore aren't you?"

"Let me up!"

I pull on her hair even harder.

"That cunt of yours is just asking for it."

Gripping the cock with one hand, I slap it against her pussy lips hard again and again.

Thwack! Thwack thwack!

She whimpers and continues to struggle. I put my knee to her wound that's still covered in its bandage and she chokes.

"Choking already? Do you need my cock in your mouth so you have something else you can choke on?"

Magda grits her teeth and her eyes shine, but she fights with her spirit nonetheless. How many times have we all found ourselves in these situations? The men who try to break us day in and day out? Only to find us surviving and coming back stronger and more numb.

I've been too easy on the girls. They've already forgotten what it could be like without us looking out for ourselves.

Pulling her hair again, I can see the roots getting red. Licking the shell of her ear, my hand goes down to dig my finger against her bandage.

"Ahhhhh!"

"That's it. Scream for me, you little whore."

I dig in again and I think I hear Mister Reeves choke.

"Ahhhh!"

Her legs tremble and she's barely holding on. Straightening up, I ram the dildo into her wet pussy and start pounding into her.

Thump. Thump. Thump.

Her hips hit the desk and it only drives me higher. I'm beginning to perspire when I pull the dildo out of her, spit on it and shove it into her ass.

"Ahhhhhh!"

"Scream for me some more. You know how I like it."

She stops screaming then. Trying to will herself to survive this invasion. My hands reach around us and start to pinch and pull her clit, my fingers slipping between her wet folds now and again. She almost falls over when her climax hits her with the dildo still in her ass.

Pulling out, the blood helps with the slide. Shoving her to the ground, I take off the strap-on and throw it at her back.

"Get out of my office, Magda. Don't question me again."

My eyes turn to Mister Reeves who has his hands clasped together in front of his crotch. I lift an eyebrow, and blow him a kiss.

"Have your man come down to take Magda. Tell him his extra pay will be her pussy. Report back to me if you see anything else suspicious around our building. I'm trusting you understand the logic behind my decisions."

Mister Reeves clears his throat and loosens his collar before he nods. "Cornell."

"Cornell."

He speaks quietly into his radio and a few minutes later, a younger gentleman comes in to gather Magda into his arms. She fights like a hellcat but his grip on her is sure as he walks out without looking at either of us.

My hands begin to unbutton my top when I ask him, "Cornell. How well versed are you in patting a woman down?"

His eyes blaze when my breasts spill out.

"I'm going to need to test you to make sure your skills are up to par."

Crooking my finger in the 'come hither' motion, Mister Reeves unbuckles his pants as he walks toward me.

Domination and control does something to me. It brings me to life more than anything else. My head of security begins to run his hand down my sides while his open fly jingles against his belt buckle.

For such a scowling man, his hands are soft and too kind for a place like this. Grabbing his shirt, I slam his lips on mine and invade his mouth with my tongue. It opens the floodgates and our clothes get strewn about as Mister Reeves walks me back against my desk. Taking his lips off me for a second, his strong hands grip me and lift my ass onto the wood.

With savagery I didn't know he had in him, he opens the fly to my pencil skirt and rips it off me, scraping my skin with the fabric along the way. Groaning, he pushes my legs apart and fingers the wetness already accumulated from the disciplinary session I had to perform in front of him.

He pulls his cock out and I can feel my pussy pulsate in anticipation. My mouth waters at the size of him but he doesn't let me look for long when he maneuvers the head of his cock up and down my wet lips, teasing me.

"You're here to get a job done, Mister-"

He slams his cock into me before I can finish the sentence, the size of him taking my breath away with how he deliciously stretches me. What I thought was a gentle lover quickly turns into a savage beast pounding against me like a man exorcising his inner demons.

I take it. I take every bit of it with pleasure because I need to exorcize my demons too. The push and pull, the scratches and the biting all bring the sensation higher and higher.

"You shouldn't feel this good."

"Because I'm a whore?"

He rams into me so hard, the skin on my ass feels like it's getting ripped from the wooden desk beneath me. Moaning, I almost forget my question until he answers me at the most inopportune time.

"Because I don't need to get addicted to something that will end up burning me alive."

His hips twist on the next thrust and it hits my clit in just the right angle. His warm hand clamps over my neck as he slams his mouth on mine, mimicking everything his dick is doing to me with his tongue.

A sharp pain on my nipple sends me over the edge and the beast above me groans in pain.

"Fuck."

With a few more hard thrusts, Mister Reeves pulls his dick out and cums all over my stomach. I watch in fascination as his scowl deepens while his hand glistens with our combined juices.

When the last jet of cum lands on me, Mister Reeves pushes my shoulders down against the table and sticks his dick back inside.

Leaning in just enough so his release doesn't touch his top, his hot breath against the crook of my neck sends shivers down my spine.

"Don't ask this of me again, Mistress. You might not like the result."

Purring, I leave his last statement hanging in the air, close my eyes, and let myself enjoy him slowly thrust into me until his cock dies down.

Chapter Twelve

MAGDA

I feel hot, hot everywhere. I can't escape the heat and I'm suffocating from something I can't see. It's dark, too dark. Where the hell am I?

"Ahhhhh!"

My leg throbs and I want to kill someone. I'm scratching at my own skin, trying to wake myself up but it doesn't work. Shaking my head side to side, I hit something hard and jerk, falling off the bed.

I'm breathing hard, trying to figure out what the hell just happened. Looking around, I see that I'm back in my room. Wasn't I just in Erdene's office? Fucking hell! She's done it to me again. These mind games of hers kill me.

The trauma of the assault has plagued my dreams and invaded my sleep for all my adult life. My young experience has sculpted my existence – my choices – my decisions. The good and bad.

Then, one night, by the grace of God, or maybe because of

me cutting his brake lines, he was in a fatal car crash on his way home. That was the last time I saw him.

Little did I know I was trading one prison for another.

By that time, I realized that cutting was an escape. Whether it was myself, something or someone else, it was my release from the humiliation and pain. The emotions that continue to plague me like a disease, refuse to let me heal. Time has done nothing. Whoever says time heals all wounds fucking lied.

When I met Erdene, I knew she was as broken as I was. In life we are *all* broken, it just depends on if we choose to rise up from it or let ourselves burn in the ashes. And to me, Erdene shone as the brightest damn phoenix I have ever seen. I can't help but be a moth drawn to her flame.

Becoming a debt owed to the men my father had dealings with didn't become my grave as I had imagined. Erdene did what she had to, to fight for all of us. And she rose like the queen she became.

She took me in and built me back up into something whole – well, as whole as I could be. I came to her broken. That was accepted, almost taken as a badge of honor around these parts. In being broken, she could accept me. Hurting me was easy for her, it was the putting back together again, she struggled with.

None of us girls can be put back together again. We can never be who we were before. Erdene, in my eyes, is a fixer. She's the glue for all of us girls' broken parts. My pieces stay together simply to keep hers intact.

At one point, after the change in regime, I thought about trying to have a normal life. But my head is too fucked up for that. The scars I bear are not from nights on the street when I was forced to survive before entering the House, they are from my nights of darkness with my switchblade.

Just the thought of it makes my body tense up with antici-pation. The cut is a bloodletting - a feeling of release that I need.

Thinking I have redeemed myself working for Erdene is bullshit. *I am bullshit.* It took Mister Spence throwing me over the precipice of fear to prove that I am nothing more than a fractured girl who needs help picking the pieces back up.

History just repeats itself. There is no hope here. There isn't any hope anywhere. We are all haunting this House, living a half life until our time is up or until we are used up. The jobs we get in the basement are like a drug with a temporary high.

With thoughts like these filling my mind, I'm positive before this night is over there will be new scars adorning my skin. My eyes dart to the side of the room where I keep it hidden. Fuck it.

Getting up off the floor, I walk over and grab it like an addict. I shouldn't even have this in my room but I do. Temptation pulsates in the back of my mind especially in vulnerable moments like these. Hell, I shouldn't be left alone in a room, but I am.

The tip of the blade is so scintillating as it nicks my skin. The weight of the handle in my hand is a comfort I know well, one I constantly seek for reassurance. Slowly, as it drags across my arm, I hiss at the sting of pain - pain that releases from me inside and out. I can feel my nerves start to settle. *Just one more, one more slice.* Except when you're addicted, once is never enough for your vice.

I can hear the door open, and normally, I would hide – ashamed by my act. But today, I've been battered emotionally, mentally, and physically. I don't have the strength to be embarrassed.

I hear her heels tapping across the floor. Her sigh of disapproval, the clicking of her teeth. Looking up at her, all I can offer her is all I have left – a very tattered psyche.

That will have to be good enough for now.

ERDENE

I had high hopes for her. I thought she'd be the one who would be able to stand by my side through thick and thin. If one moment can bring her down to this, how can she stand up against the men that can potentially take over the house? They won't hesitate to make us all slaves and cumdumpsters for their men, choosing younger flesh to peddle through the House of Eden.

Kicking her, I force her attention on me. "Get up."

She blankly looks at me, blinking slowly. She's lost in her internal turmoil and pain. The memories are bombarding her too hard today. *Tsking* in disgust, I turn toward her door and signal for Nolan to come back inside. He radioed in for assistance when he couldn't get her out of her head. He tackled the blade out of her grip a few times but like a zombie she scrambled to get it back against her skin.

"Nolan, I need you to subdue her." I command.

"What do you mean? She's just on the floor cutting herself."

Turning to him, I grab the front of his shirt and snarl. "I need you to fuck her back into reality. I need her to break away from that which haunts her. *Your cock is needed for service for the good of the House.*"

Nolan looks at me astonished. I know how it sounds. But that is the life of a lady of the House of Eden. We've all been through different levels of hell and only certain things are able to bring us back. With Magda, it's always someone fucking her with certain phrases.

One set breaks her and another enrages her enough to bring her back.

Pulling Nolan down, my words whisper against his ears. Shoving him away from me, I walk out the door and shut them both inside.

Chapter Thirteen

MISTER REEVES

"Jinder, I need you to look someone up for me."

"What the hell do I look like, your gopher?" The shit that comes out of this man's mouth.

"Shut the hell up and turn your computer on." I snap.

"Fucker. My computer is always on, you know this. Alright, what am I looking for?"

"I need to look up a patron's file. His name is Cooper Hale."

Click click click.

"Why does his name sound familiar?" he questions out loud to mostly himself.

"I don't know but I had the same feeling when he came through the door. I don't recognize his face, but my gut tells me something is up."

"You sure that's his name?"

"It's what's signed up on the file at the House. Patrons are required two forms of ID and a couple of references to vouch." It's what I've been informed about.

"Does he have blond hair and a scar under his left eye?"

"No."

"Huh. Wrong guy. Spell his name for me."

"C-O-O-P-E-R." I enunciate each letter clearly.

"Alright, and Hale probably isn't spelled any other way. Let me see."

Click click click.

"Nah. The guy doesn't have any sort of rap sheet other than an accusation of bribery."

"Alright. Thanks Jinder."

Hanging up the phone my mind turns over everything I've learned. There's just something about the way the patron carries himself and walks that sparks a long forgotten memory in the back of my mind. I can't put my finger on it.

The evening continues on without much of anything happening. After our little tryst in the office, Erdene has been assigning me behind the computer screen to keep an eye on things. What she does when she's out of the House, nobody knows and nobody questions.

Thoughts of wetting my dick inside her tight pussy make my cock twitch. *Fuck.* Rubbing my hand down my face, I try to forget the phantom feeling of her cunt. I know she is trouble. I should have never taken the offer. *Who the fuck says no to that, though?* Dammit.

"Boss."

The image of me ramming myself inside her tight hole fractures when my radio comes on.

"Yeah." My voice is gruffer than I'd like and I wince.

"You need to come see this." The sound of his voice tells me I won't like what I find.

"Where are you located?" My mind is already envisioning the perimeter of the place.

"North side of the building in the back by the dumpsters." His voice crackles over the radio in response.

With one last glance at the screen, I make sure nothing else is amiss before exiting the office. It's located far away from the Mistress and that's a blessing in disguise. I won't be able to concentrate if I smell her scent all day. Shutting and locking the door behind me, I walk across the hall and double check the open doors to see if anyone needs anything. I nod at Jessi in the front lobby and my men before going through the doors. Walking around the outside perimeter, I catch sight of some of my men on the nearby buildings rooftops.

Beau can be seen leaning into his collar right before the crackle of the radio comes on in my earpiece. "Look under the dumpster. I saw something through my scope. No one else has been seen walking to or from the area since my shift."

"Got it."

Rounding around the back, the two dumpsters sit side by side, their lids neatly closed. For such an establishment, Erdene keeps a tight ship inside and out. How one woman is able to maintain that much control is beyond my understanding. The girls all fear her and take everything she says as law. There's a story here, one I'm sure will unfold over time.

It's during this very thought that I see it.

At first glance it looks like a shoe that probably fell out of a trash bag. On closer inspection, it's an actual foot still attached to a woman's shoe. The stench isn't that powerful yet, letting me know it's fresh. The blood barely oozes out, which makes me think the body was frozen before it was dumped - or perhaps frozen before it was chopped.

My eyes scan the surroundings as I report my findings to the men. Looking around one more time, I stand and open the dumpster lid. Nothing is amiss. Not even the smell of petrified flesh. Why would there only be a foot left behind if someone was trying to dump a body?

Who's body is it?

"Somebody bring a bag down and grab this shit." I yell out.

"You got it, boss."

Walking back into the front of the building, I grab Jessi's attention.

"Call your Mistress. We have a problem."

Chapter Fourteen

JESSI

"Call your Mistress." His masculine voice makes me snap my head in his direction in question.

We have a problem. I swivel my chair around so he won't see me roll my eyes. When *don't* we have a problem around here? I can't remember the last day where everything ran smoothly without anyone getting hurt.

I've had to *gently* remind Mr. Reeves three times today that I do not work for him. I hate to be more aggressive with him, however, I have my own duties to perform and pouring his coffee is not on that list.

My eyes narrow on him and his eyes narrow on mine in challenge. I still don't know if I can trust the guy as far as I can throw him. But Erdene made him head of security and that says something.

Clearing my throat, I get up.

Being too stern would make it a hostile environment in the main office, which will end up being a pain in the ass for us both when Erdene catches wind of it. Dealing with her psychotic rage is already hard enough, though it's decreased over the past few years. But, I never know from day to day if I am going to get maternal Erdene or the 'I'm going to eat your face off and wear your skin as a suit' Erdene.

I shake my head to dislodge my opinions from inside my skull. Just having those thoughts alone, could get you killed around here.

Grabbing the phone off the hook, I dial the Mistress' office number from memory. This place is seriously outdated. I could have messaged her on the computer, but I'm feeling petty and want to be dramatic.

Ring. Ring.

Erdene finally picks up. "Why are you calling me on the phone? You could have just messaged me."

My eyes narrow again on the man before me. "Mister Reeves needs to talk to you."

"Why didn't he call me?" I can hear the exasperation in her voice. Understandably so. I'd be exasperated too. He has fucking legs, he could just walk in there and find her if it is so damn important.

"What does he need to talk to me about?" she finally asks.

"I don't know. He says we have a problem." *Don't shoot the messenger.* "He seems to think I am at his beck and call." I automatically grimace once the words leave my mouth. I realize how overly petty it sounds but at this point, I can' take it back.

Mister Reeves gives me a glare but doesn't say a word. *His eyes say enough.*

The sound of her fingernails clicking on whatever surface she is near echoes through the phone speaker. "Anything else?"

"No, Mistress. I apologize." I can practically hear a pin drop with how silent it is on the other side. She's going to kill me. The longer the moments pass, the more my heart beats into my throat.

"You have nothing to apologize for. He should've called me himself."

The line goes dead.

~

MR. REEVES

Waiting for Erdene to get here, I mentally go over clues I might have missed. I know the girls didn't stash the body. Assuming the Mistress isn't stupid enough to shit where she eats — that is kill someone and dump their body parts at her *own* place — then someone is trying to set her up.

Jessi is probably pissed off, but she can shove it down her throat. I'm not here to play games. If she continues to rub me the wrong way, she'll find me stuffing her pert little mouth with my cock. Every single woman in the House of Eden is a temptation. Looking at the lobby girl now, my mind is going places it shouldn't. The thought of those plump lips surrounding me while those sly eyes look up at me - my dick is practically bursting at the seams, despite the situation at hand.

Maybe I just want to erase the memory of Erdene out of my mind. Fucking the Mistress under her command is one thing. The secretary? That is one mistake I can't make.

Why do I feel this growing attraction to the head mistress? Is it her air of authority? A viper in a den of the innocent? But what whore is innocent, really?

Jessi's eyes narrow on me again almost as if she can read my mind and my pants grow a little tighter. What is it about this house? Maybe it's the fact that Jessi looks like she's going to gut me from the neck down right now.

Flashes of Erdene and her quick aggression cools my desire.

Hitting this could cost me my life.

Erdene doesn't fuck around when it comes to her girls from what I've witnessed. She's also stated as much. This woman is her secretary for a reason. My guess is because she has no interest in the dealings of flesh. Shit, I have no reason to fuck anyone in this damn place. I don't need the liability of having to protect someone else I end up caring about.

I still haven't made it up to you, Celia.

I'm not willing to lose anyone else. So, yes, secretary dagger-eyes is off limits.

Get your head back in the game, Reeves.

Going over the details of what I found one more time, I try to take note of everything that stands out.

The foot is larger like a man's size. But I'm not an expert on feet. The strangest question to me is: *Why a foot?*

Is this a warning? Of course, it is. What's the person or persons trying to say? What the hell can a foot symbolize at a house of ill repute? If there had been a head with the lips sewn shut, the message might have been to keep your mouth shut. If you steal from people, it's your hand or fingers that get cut off. So what did this *foot* signify? Is there a prior client who had a foot fetish?

"Fancy meeting you here," Erdene's sultry voice shakes me out of my reverie.

I am so deep in thought; I didn't hear walk over despite the stilettos she always wears. Her words say one thing, but her eyes say another. The Mistress of the house is a very complicated and layered woman.

"So, what seems to be the problem? Jessi said it was urgent." She doesn't sound concerned whatsoever.

My mind's eye flashes back to the severed limb while my sights take in the woman before me. *She shouldn't be this attractive. Especially for a woman who easily punishes her girls against desks.* "Has there been any recent clients coming in with a foot fetish?"

Erdene raises an eyebrow but doesn't say a word.

Grabbing her elbow, I watch as her nostrils flare and her pupils change size but it doesn't stop me from leaning in. "Seems we found something behind the dumpsters. How about I take you out there and see if you recognize anything?"

The smile she plasters on her face is sinister, right before it morphs into something fake.

"Lead the way, *Cornell.*" The sound of my name on her lips makes my cock twitch but I ignore it as I drag her out the front doors and around to the back.

Some of my boys are already there with black trash bags, gathering what I assume are the other pieces to the puzzle.

"I think we got everything, Boss."

"Do we have a head?" I ask.

"The men and I looked through the dumpsters twice. Nothing. It was the only missing part."

"Any tell tale marks?"

Ace, one of my younger guys, walks to the group and starts asking them the same questions. Wells nods his head and reopens a bag, reaches in and grabs the foot again with his gloved hand.

In my periphery, I observe the Mistress' reactions to all this. She doesn't even bat an eye which brings even more questions to my mind.

"There's a small tattoo under the second toe." Ace hands me a glove and I put it on. Turning the foot around, sure enough there it is - a small tattoo of a star.

"Recognize this?" I question Erdene.

"Aria."

"Aria." Is she really only going to give me only a name?

Narrowing my eyes at her, Erdene's smile broadens. It's so out of place for this moment that my mind files her as a suspect.

"She left when I took over. She didn't want to be one of the girls in the House anymore. In my moment of weakness, I let her go. None of us have heard from her since." Her head tilts as she eyes the severed foot with scrutiny. "Though it seems, *someone* wanted to bring her home."

"Indeed, it does." Without taking my eyes off her, I call for Wells to take the foot back. "I'm going to need more information on this Aria."

"Of course." She replies nonchalantly.

Why is she so calm? Her eyes are on me but I can't read her thoughts or expressions. Without removing my gaze from her, I address the men. "Clean this shit up guys. Report back to me when things are done."

"On it, Boss."

"I don't need the cops snooping around this place." I tell them.

The sound of shuffling, trash bags and boots can be heard as my men quickly do what I say.

Erdene and I stand toe to toe, continuing to stare each other down - or maybe it's just from my side. *What's going on in that head of hers?*

When the men leave the vicinity with the body parts, my eyes land on the exposed column of her neck. Her breathing is even, not even a hitch. What is it about her that makes me feel like I want to break her in two and see what she's hiding?

Chapter Fifteen

He wants to be the one.

So does Alexander.

So do many of the men who walk through the doors to the House of Eden. Alexander is the only plaything I left standing, but he doesn't know that. His son was fun while he lasted.

I let Cornell play his little game of dominance, let him think he has the upper hand. It's the only way to get their guard down while I collect everything I need to use against them later. Men like him haven't been around women like us, the ones who have been pushed to the point of no return - to the point of having nothing to lose.

Since coming to the top and taking over the house, losing is not something I plan to do. *Not in this game.*

Whoever is sending us this message is going to pay up and they won't see us coming.

Cornell steps toward me until I hit the wall of the building with my back, essentially trapping me. It's a power play. Men always seem to use the same tactics. Seductively looking at him,

I can still remember how his cock felt between my legs. It was a power move on my part in the office, one I had to make quickly.

When his arms come up against the wall on either side of me, I tilt my head back and slightly part my lips. He smells of masculine musk and the sun. His eyes dilate into dark orbs but he doesn't take the bait. Alexander didn't take the bait initially either. When one of his hands comes down and trails a finger down my cheek, a few things click into place. Oh, he's not a rookie to this game either.

His voice has lowered in octaves but his eyes continue to bore into mine. "Why didn't you seem surprised to find a chopped up body? What secrets have you been hiding?"

His fingers continue to trail across my jaw and back again until it travels over my chin, whispering against my lower lip.

Lowering my lashes, I peek at him from under them. "A lady never tells, Mister Reeves."

How long is this game going to last? I need to check in with my girls and see what really happened with Aria. One of them has to have kept contact with her, it's how women are.

He raises an eyebrow and suppresses a smirk. "Back to Mister Reeves now? What did I do?"

My eyes flash at him for a second. His question brings up memories I don't need right now. The phantom memory of my hands around a bloodied neck makes my fingers tingle. My breasts feel heavy with want - for sex or bloodshed, I'm yet uncertain.

"What are we doing right now, Cornell?"

"You need to tell me what I need to know so I can do my job correctly."

"You know all you need to know."

He raises an eyebrow and leans in. Our mouths are but a breath apart when he groans against my lips. My hands continue to squeeze his balls and slightly twist. If this is a dick swinging contest, then it's about time I take out the competition to end this game here and now.

"Cornell." My voice comes out breathy, wanton, as I watch him begin to breathe deeply with each subsequent squeeze I give. "I'm going to need you to find out what's happening behind my house, and find out quickly. I'm not a patient woman, not when it comes to this." Pulling him against me by the balls, I can see him grind his teeth subtly. "And when it's all said and done, then maybe I'll let you cum like a good little boy. If you deserve it."

Licking the shell of his ear, I shove him off me. The taste of him still lingers on my tongue as I turn on my heels and head back to the front of the building without giving him the satisfaction of looking back.

Chapter Sixteen

ERDENE

"We shouldn't be doing this. You need to stop fucking coming around." Alexander growls behind me but doesn't stop what he's doing.

He continues to plow his dick into my wet, aching hole, making me have to try harder to not make a sound in this underground garage.

"Fuck. This pussy is going to kill me one day. You need to stay the fuck away from me!"

The sound of flesh slapping against flesh echoes lightly as he squeezes my breasts and pinches my nipples, forcing me to fight for control over my noises. *The rat bastard.*

"It was you who called me over." I tell between thrusts.

His hand goes around my neck from behind, his hips pushing me harder against the hood of his car. Trailing a wet tongue over the back of my neck, Alexander huskily breathes against the shell of my ear. "It was you who brought this fucking pussy to me like a damn gift to be opened." *Thrust.* "Every." *Thrust.* "Single." *Thrust.* "Time."

Biting my bottom lip, my pussy clenches at his ferocity. Turning my head to the side for a more comfortable position, I breathe out, "Your dick isn't that good anyway."

He chuckles against the back of my head right before he growls and pummels into me with brute strength. The pain of my hips hitting the hood of his vehicle drives my pleasure higher, the grill in front of his car rubs against my clit in all the right ways.

"Whores don't need good dick, they just need to have their holes filled up to keep them happy."

Asshole.

A few more quick thrusts and he pulls out, cumming all over the ground next to us. I'm left bereft, my pleasurable high crashing down quickly.

"You said my dick wasn't that good anyway. Get your orgasms from someone else." Why does the last statement come out through gritted teeth?

Ring! Ring! A cell phone shrills loudly.

Alexander scrambles to fix his pants and zip them up before grabbing the vibrating phone out of his pocket. I can see his sweet wife's face lighting up the screen and I smirk.

"Hey, honey." Oh, look at how his voice changes.

"Hey, where are you?" I can hear her on the other line in the now quiet of the garage.

The talent this man has in controlling his breathing fascinates me.

"Just leaving the office. Did you need anything?"

"No, I just missed you and wanted to hear your voice." She says with a whine.

He chuckles like a good husband, shoves me off the hood of his car and proceeds to walk toward the driver's side door without any further acknowledgement. I grind my teeth down while I fix my clothes. The roar of the engine comes on and Alexander slowly pulls out the underground garage, leaving me in the dust.

Grabbing the phone out of my bag, I scroll through my messages to make sure the one I sent the other day is still there - and it is. It just hasn't been opened and read yet.

"Poor Alexander." I say under my breath.

I couldn't care less when the explosion happens. The time for the fall of his empire is close and that's all that matters. Walking in my heels toward my vehicle, I get in and let myself sink into the seat.

His dick really isn't that good. So why does my pussy pulsate like he's still inside of me? I need to cut this shit between us off and in a hurry.

Pulling out the garage, the rays of the sun temporarily blinds me as I pull onto the streets.

Ring! Ring!

The old school ring of my phone goes off and I hit the button to take it and put it on speaker.

"What do you need?" I answer.

"I see this is the way you treat everyone."

"Mister R-"

"Don't. Look, something came up at the House. I need you here. Now."

"On my way." Hanging up, I step on the gas and take the next turn.

I managed to not run over anyone on the way back and the moment I step through the front doors is the moment I feel it. "Who's missing?"

"She was last seen about thirty minutes ago when a client left her room. That's all the girls told me. The cameras showed her exiting toward the basement. A few moments later, she comes back up and there's been a hitch in the video. Like someone suddenly put it on a loop. That's what alerted me. The men are still out there scouring the area."

I knew it. Dammit! The men weren't put in place fast enough. There's been an infiltrator in our midst this whole time, right under our noses. Fuck!

"Mister Reeves. To my office." His face scowls but I ignore it. "Everyone else, have one man with you at all times. Continue to take clients but have your man stand outside the door. You guys will be partnering up until further notice."

"I don't have enough men for the amount of women in this House."

Turning a snarl at his face, I emphasize my words carefully. "Then have your men figure. It. Out."

Leaving the lobby, I walk directly to my office knowing that my head of security is right behind my heels. The moment the door closes is the moment Mister Reeves grabs my arm. My body reacts automatically and my knee comes up, getting blocked by his thigh. My fist comes next and he grabs my wrist right before it makes contact.

We're both breathing hard but not saying a word.

"I'm going to need you to keep your wits about you, *Mistress*."

My eyes narrow at his emphasis but I keep my mouth shut. I've almost reached my limit with men and their condescending tones. He scowls and inhales deeply, flaring his nostrils right before he shoves me away like I've burned him.

"Your girls informed me that the name of the one missing is Möngömaa."

My chest constricts and my heart speeds up. Besides Magda, Möngömaa has been here the longest. Turning away from him to walk to my desk, I ask him my question so he doesn't see any expression I may have on my face.

"And how long has she been missing?"

"At this point, going on forty-five minutes. What can you tell me about her? What do I need to know?" He's prodding, but I stay on my course.

"She's a lady of the House. Besides myself and Magda, she's the other one that's been here the longest."

"Anything else?" I can feel the heat of him against me from behind and it makes the hair on the back of my neck stand on end.

In a game like this, it's wise to not show any signs of fear - especially when a predator is nearby.

Turning slowly, I make sure to rub my ass against his crotch before I face him. "No. There's nothing else." He doesn't need to know about what we do down below. He gives me a suspicious look and thins his lips.

"In order for me to fully take care of this House of yours, Mistress, I'm going to need you to be honest with me. What do you know that can help us find our missing commodity?"

"Men hate us and men want us. Each client on that roster has become a suspect. I don't know what else you want from me. We've obviously been infiltrated by some sort of rivalry or there is some sort of vendetta."

"Why would a whore gain herself a vendetta from someone?"

"You're a man, you tell me? Maybe he lost his marriage by shoving his dick down the wrong hole too much. Maybe his wife doesn't want to be pissed on. You tell me."

His lips quirk but the scowl remains. A few beats of silence and Mister Reeves lifts the radio on his collar to whisper, "Go through the clientele list and have everyone one of them investigated the next time they step foot in this place. One man to every three girls. The rest of you keep looking for clues."

Mister Reeves turns and walks away. As he grabs the handle

to the door, he looks over his shoulder. "You've got a package in the front with Jessi. I'll probably come by later to give you the updates."

The door closes with a whoosh and my anger grows. Who the hell has the audacity to come into *my* home and take one of *my* girls? Stomping over to the other side of the desk, my fingers fly across the keyboard to message Jessi.

> Erdene: I need one of the girls in the basement in the next thirty minutes.

> Jessi: Yes, Mistress. You also have a package.

> Erdene: Bring it in and do not forward any more calls until I tell you.

> Jessi: Yes, Mistress.

A soft knock at the door and Jessi pokes her head in, bringing a plain medium rectangular box with her.

"I stepped out to go pee and when I got back, this was on my desk addressed to you."

"Thank you."

After handing it to me, she exits just as quietly as she came. The brown wrapping is plain. The weight of the box is lighter than I anticipated. Walking back over to my desk, I unwrap it and open the lid.

The finger that lies on top of the cushion makes it look like a damn precious offering. Lifting it between my fingertips, I place the box on the desk and examine it. The light whitish scar along the inside of the second knuckle tells me exactly who it is.

Möngömaa.

My anger skyrockets and my eyes burn. Taking a few deep

breaths in and out, I place the finger back into the box, walk around the computer and message Jessi to bring Mister Reeves back into the office.

Hang on, Möngömaa. We're coming to find you and we're not leaving anyone who did you wrong alive to tell the tale.

Chapter Seventeen

THE UNKNOWN

Kidnapping her is easier than it should have been. These women never pay attention to their surroundings. Especially a house of whores who think they are more than what they are. They think they are untouchable because of the patrons that come through. How stupid can these women be? She'll find out, *they all will*, that I get anything I want.

She walks in and out of the shops with an air of superiority. I don't know why I am assigned the job, and I don't care. All I care about is that I get paid when the job is done so I can move on. It took a while to become part of the clientele and a sizable amount of cash to get two strangers to agree to be used as references.

But here I am, in the heart of the whore house.

As soon as she walks by the entrance of the hallway in the back of the whorehouse, I grab her with an ether cloth. *Too easy. Much too easy.* No struggles, no screams. The only sound that can be heard are the moans and groans from the other rooms hiding everything that's happening. It's easy finding a restroom with a window just big enough to toss her body out.

The new security system the head whore put in place is easy to hack into. All that is required is perfect timing.

"Have a wonderful day! We hope to see you back and the House of Eden soon."

"Thank you, my dear. Always a pleasure. You ladies really do take care of your clients. I'll make sure to recommend you to everyone I know."

"Lovely." Waving off the front desk girl, I leisurely walk past the two security guards at the door and to my car.

The clientele has been coming and going more today than last week. Using all the movement around us to hide my change in direction, I quickly grab and drag the body of the whore toward a darker corner. The camera's pointing this way have been put in a loop for a thirty-minute span.

"Hey! This is my second time coming here. Is there any one of the ladies with specialties I need to know about?"

The amount of debauchery that goes on in this whore house fascinates me. Easing into the conversation like it's a question I get asked everyday, I smirk and tip my head toward the entrance. "I haven't had the chance to explore them all, but if you ask the front desk lady, she may be able to direct you to the perfect girl."

His eyes gleam and gloss over before he smiles and waves goodbye.

Following a group of men that just exited the front, I walk around the side to find where I parked my vehicle.

The hum of the engine starting makes my dick twitch, as I strategically watch the direction of all the cars leaving. Pulling my vehicle out with one of the cars entering, I quickly find a more covered location to park the car and throw the limp body into the trunk. She slowly wakes up right as I shove her upper body in and a quick fist to the face knocks her right out again. She does have some fight in her, I'll give her that. Most girls wouldn't rouse this quickly. But a whore her size is still no match for me. Shutting the trunk, I pretend to pull behind the next car in line, waiting for about five minutes before pulling out onto the street like a patron who changed his mind last minute.

Ring! Ring!

My finger hits the answer button. "Haren."

"Did you get what I need?"

"Close enough."

"What do you mean close enough? You were paid for the head Mistress."

"Trust the process." Hanging up, I internally laugh at the asshole who hired me. If he is that desperate to get things done, he should have done it himself.

The classical music that comes through my speakers soothes my soul as I continue to drive toward our destination. Getting her to the dilapidated warehouse is easy enough. Taking the long way is necessary as I circle around the block a few extra times as a precaution in case I'm being followed. My intel tells me that some of the guys the head whore hired have a past.

Pulling up behind the warehouse, I take off my jacket and toss it on the passenger seat. No point in getting it dirty, after all. Popping the trunk open, I exit the driver side and start rolling my sleeves up.

"Alright. Let's see what we have here."

Lifting the trunk, I take a good look at the whore. She looks Asian, kind of stocky. Not too bad on the eyes. Maybe I'll play with her later once I do what needs to be done. Watching her chest slowly rise and fall, I grab her tit and squeeze it. She moans but doesn't fully wake just yet. Tossing her over my shoulder, I shut the trunk with a thud and whistle all the way to her new extended stay room.

The basement of this place is cold and rank but perfect for what I need to do. Tossing her down, the crack from her forehead hitting the pavement makes my face sour. So much for a pretty face. Whistling again, I start to chain her wrists, tying them together and then walk over to the pulley to lift her up toward the ceiling. *Oops.* Too high. Rolling the pulley back down a few inches so her toes can grace the floor, I lock the mechanism in place.

Her tits do look so lovely like this. I am but a selfish man. Walking over to her, my hands come up to caress her breasts when suddenly she knees me in the gut.

The pain turns me on as I land a slap on her face. She bares her teeth and begins struggling until my fists hit her face making her swing a little back and forth. A fighter, this one. I like it.

Walking over to my chest of tools, I grab one of the hunting knives my father gave me before he passed away.

A groan echoes behind me and I smile. Oh, I do like this one very much.

"Wh-"

She groans again and my pants get tighter. What is it about a woman under your power? Especially one that doesn't know she is.

"The fuck?"

The rattle and clinking of the chains get louder and louder the more she struggles. Turning I watch the way her breasts bounce and the way her hips move. There's something about her. She's not a typical whore. Without skipping a beat, the moment I get close enough, the little minx brings her legs up for a kick. Blocking it with my forearm, my hand fists the hilt firmly, swiping up to make her gasp and swinging down to impale her skin.

"Ahhh!"

Groaning, I rub the front of my crotch, watching the way she swings with the handle of my father's knife sticking out of her.

She passes out straight away, bleeding like a stuffed pig. How disappointing. I don't want her to die that easily, where's the fun in that? I still need to lure out the head mistress so I can finish this stupid job.

Pulling out the smelling salts I use for occasions like this, I hold it under her nose. She jerks and the chains clink but her head lolls again. Oh, this just will not do. I don't like to be ignored.

Pulling the blade out, she whimpers. Smiling, I shove it right back into another location and gleefully listen to her scream.

~

MÜNGÖMAA

The pain is excruciating. It's drowning out all my sensible thoughts on how I ended up in this position in the first place. One minute I'm coming up from the basement, walking toward the hallway and the next - darkness. I can feel the blade going through my skin, making me scream bloody murder. The way this asshole tied me to the damn ceiling has me slipping on the blood that's accumulated below me. The dark, dank room I'm currently in is drifting in and out of my vision.

"Ahhhh!"

The blade enters me again, making me squeeze my eyes shut. When I open them back up, I realize it's the blood running down my forehead and into my eyes that's making my vision blurry.

Falling in and out of semi-consciousness, I feel the hard, coldness of the concrete before I hear the *thump* of my body go down on it. Darkness kisses and welcomes me into its embrace. A peaceful moment found in the nothingness. The next thing I remember is the smell of ammonia assaulting my senses. My eyes fly open, as my stomach heaves up my breakfast that my daughter so lovingly made me. That seemed like eons ago. Wait a minute. She died eons ago.

Where am I?

Who is this person? The guy is still holding the smelling salts he put under my nose. The reality of what's happening comes crashing into me, making my stomach churn. The stranger dodges just in time as vomit spews from my mouth. Trying to lift my head up, the room starts spinning like I've been given something - the way the old regime used to give us things in order to make us cry less when the patrons came in. I tilt my head to the side to see if it helps - it doesn't.

My voice comes out scratchy. "Water." I desperately need to get the taste of bile from my mouth.

"*Tsk. Tsk. Tsk.*" I can't see his face, but the clicking of his tongue is telling me I'm shit out of luck.

Looking down at my bleeding abdomen, the world spinning doesn't prevent me from seeing the ugly sight clearly. "I'm going to die." That is as blunt as I can put it. A reminder to me, and a reminder to whoever this guy is in front of me. Despite it being said out loud, my cloudy mind is still trying to grasp at the facts.

My lower half feels numb. My nerve endings are dying. Now, I'm not a medical professional, and I'm not even sure they can die, but in my mind it makes sense. But then again, my mind is starting to stray off the deep end I will admit. It feels almost surreal but so real at the same time. I can see these little nerves that resemble worker ants with hard hats, and the boss turns to look at his other nerve worker ants and says, "Okay boys, you can stop doing your job. We are going to die now."

Whoosh. More vomit spews out of my mouth, increasing the taste of acrid bile on my tongue.

Oof.

"Ahhhh!" A boot to my stomach brings me back to reality. "What the fuck?" I scream. Maybe I shouldn't have but it's too late now.

"I said your name three times." He shrugs.

He has? I didn't hear him. His voice is squeaky. Not at all what you would expect for a muscled up bad guy. I mean, that's what he is right? That's what's happening? I'm just a whore after all, what do I know? It must be the steroids that make this guy so big. Why is his damn voice so squeaky though? I bet his dick is tiny. That makes me giggle.

He gives me a look, like I'm crazy. So what if I am? "Well?" He asks impatiently.

Well, what? I don't know what the fuck he wants. Hell, I'm still trying to catch my breath and revive my little army of nerve ants. What's his problem?

He glares at me, probably waiting on my response. I have no fucking clue what's going on but when I get out of here, it wont matter because this fucker will be dead. But since we're here, might as well ask. "What's up, small time?"

His face screws up in rage. "What the fuck did you just call me?"

Smiling was the last thing I did before my world became drowned out in pain.

Chapter Eighteen

"Jinder, can you see if you can find the source of who cut into our security system?" I'm constantly owing this fucker.

"Crapshoot already?"

"Shut up and just find out for me." I growl.

"Pfft, it was already pinged to my system. Just didn't mention anything because I figured you guys already had a handle on it."

"Dammit, Jinder!" I yell.

"Look, it's not my job, not my problem. I'm sending you the IP address, but you probably can't do anything with it."

Of course, he knows this. So, what's the fucking point?

Growling, my fist grips the cell phone in my hand harder than it should. From the dismembered body to now this. What game have we been caught up in? I end the call without any warning, and storm into the Mistress' office.

"Mister Reeves!" Erdene exclaims.

Watching her eyes blaze my direction from behind the

computer, she gracefully gets up in her indignation and comes around the desk. Blocking any more of her movements, I back her up until she's caged between my body and the desk, bringing my nose right up to hers. "I'm going to need you to tell me what you're hiding."

Her pupils dilate but her face never changes. "Cornell. Why would you think I'm hiding anything?" The smell of her minty breath reminds me of her taste.

"There are bodies left in pieces and girls are getting picked off. There is *something* I'm missing in all this. Something you're not telling me."

Her chest sticks out until it hits mine and the soft swell of her breast presses in all the right ways. "There are plenty of jealous and angry men who have been shunned from this place that you can choose from. Pick one and investigate them, *Mister Reeves*."

Leaning into her some more, her leg is forced to hike up so that her ass sits on her desk to make room. "I'm going to have to ask you to narrow that list down for me, *Mistress*."

"I love the way my name sounds coming out of your mouth."

This woman right here will leave me burning at the stake if it means she gets her way, I can see it now. She follows no rules but her own, while we're all floundering around her trying to figure out what her rules are.

The question that I always come back to, despite what has happened in the past few days, burns in the back of my mind like a fresh wound. "What goes on in that basement of yours?" Why was that whore seen coming out of the basement and then never again? Why was she not taken from any other location but that one? Why is there never more than one girl that goes down there at a time? There's never a set schedule either.

Why are there no security cameras down there?

The longer we stare at each other, the more the tension and magnetism in the room builds up. The Mistress is a dangerous woman, in more ways than one. "This basement of yours -"

She slams her mouth onto mine and my thoughts scatter. That is, until the shrill of a phone ringing breaks the confusion.

Ring! Ring!

Shoving me off her, she reaches back and grabs her cell phone. "Yes?"

"You had to do it, didn't you?" The male voice on the other line makes my body tense up. Who is this fucker and why is he calling her?

"Alexander." Her voice comes out in a sultry purr and my fists ball up.

Grabbing the phone, I turn off the speaker and bring it up to my ear. "I'm going to need you to stop calling. Whatever relationship you think you had with the Mistress ends here. If I hear your voice again, I'm going to find you and you won't like it when I do." Ending the call, I shove it back at the Mistress's chest and walk out her office to find out who the fuck this Alexander is and if he has anything to do with what's happening around here.

"Jinder, hack into the Mistress's phone and find out the location of the last call."

"Oh, we're hacking now, are we? I thought you were only doing security at this new stable gig of yours."

"Just do as you're told, for once?"

"I'm going to need you to buy me dinner first. But since I'm feeling generous right now, I already hacked into it when you mentioned the name. Sending you the information. Right... now." Jinder hangs up and I look at the message on my screen.

Alexander Jones, age thirty-six. Married with one son who is recently widowed. Business owner of about five of the major brothels in the city. *Well, that's interesting, indeed.*

What is his connection with this House?

The first thought that comes to mind makes me want to throw a fist into a wall. I shouldn't feel this way. She's not my woman, just my employer. So why does it feel like such a betrayal to hear this asshole's voice over the speaker phone talking in such familiar terms with her? Why would she be fucking her competition?

Because she's a whore.

Fuck. That's exactly why I shouldn't catch any feelings for her whatsoever. Complication city is not what I fucking need right now.

"Jinder."

"How many times are you going to call me today? I've got my own shit I need to complete," he complains.

"Fuck you. Get me surveillance on Alexander Jones. I need to know everyone he's been in contact within the last week as well as his whereabouts."

"You know. You should have just dropped the job. Might as well come back and do merc work somewhere else since you seem to love it so damn much."

"Shut your pie hole and just get that shit to me."

"You think he's connected to the guy who took her out, don't you?"

"If you would just fucking send me what I asked for, I may find out. So, get on it. Now!"

"Geez. Take that stick out of your ass, would ya?" Jinder hangs up, leaving me fuming at the blank screen.

Fucker had to bring that up, especially when I'm fired up like this. There's just something not right happening here. There are too many holes.

I'm tired of these little games the Mistress thinks she's playing.

Pulling the radio on my collar toward my mouth, I call the

men. "Have three guys by the Mistress's door. I'll be MIA for a few minutes. Anyone asks, I'm on a break."

"You got it, boss."

It's time I find out what's happening in this secret basement beneath the house of ill repute.

Chapter Nineteen

ALEXANDER

"I'm going to need you to stop calling. Whatever relationship you think you had with the Mistress ends here. If I hear your voice again, I'm going to find you and you won't like it when I do."

The call ends before I can say another word. The echoes of the man's voice in my ear grates my damn nerves.

That fucking cunt.

Did she really think it wise to allow some piece of shit to answer her phone when I call? Laughing out loud like a lunatic, I start to question my sanity when it comes to Erdene. My laughter turns into growls as I slam my phone into the cushioned chair beside me, making it bounce once - twice - and land on the carpeted floor with a thud.

Two can play at this game. Little whore thinks she got the best of me. I will destroy them both. There can only be one king on the board.

Didn't she know who she was fucking with?

Flashes of her bent over my car as I slammed into her from

behind temporarily sidetrack me. My plans to destroy all the pussy in her little den of sin will have to come to fruition earlier than anticipated. Maybe then she will learn to respect me. And maybe, just maybe - if she crawls - I will give the fucking whore a job.

As my bottom slut.

Chapter Twenty

MISTER REEVES

Going down to the basement is not what I expected. Not that I had any fucking clue what I was walking into. With Erdene, you never really fucking know what she is doing. For all I fucking know, she has a whole Underworld of midgets that lives in her basement.

Each step I take down barely makes a creak and that's the first clue that there's something shady going on down here. The building doesn't look tip-top shape. Why would the stairs not creak even once? Walking down further, I notice the smell first. The incense does nothing to mask the smell of death. Once you've smelled that smell, you never forget it. It singes not only your nose hairs but your mind, bringing forth memories that need to stay buried and forgotten.

Looking around the room, there's a table that sits in the middle of the floor. Again, they tried to cover and make it look normal, but any lay person could lift up the silk fabric like I'm currently doing and see the set in blood stains along the crevice and corners.

Erdene is a smart woman. Of course, she can say, and it might possibly be true, that this is a birthing table. After all, this is a den of females. However, that doesn't explain the morgue smell.

Unless, of course, they slaughtered all of the babies.

Erdene is vicious, but even I can't see her being *that* vicious.

Walking around the basement some more, I notice the furnishings. My past has seen many things - many things that give me quick answers. This is a punishment room. The whips and chains that hang on the wall can be chalked up to tools kept for the patrons upstairs. It's the other various instruments down here that would say otherwise. Tools with multiple uses, one of which is for various forms of torture.

None of the men have seen any of the ladies take clients down here. What other explanation, then, would there be for what I'm seeing? Is this a room specifically used for Erdene to punish her girls to keep them in line? If that is the case, then goddamn, the list of suspects just got longer.

With that in mind, I turn on my heel and head back up the steps to the main floor. But before I can make it the first step, a glint under the table catches my eye making me stop in my tracks.

Bending down, I pick up the item and continue up the stairs to head straight for the Queen's office.

The radio crackles.

The voice that comes over sounds like he's running.

"Repeat that."

"I just followed a guy that left one of the girl's rooms. He left the door shut after his exit. The girls usually leave it open to let the next client know they are available. She never opened the door."

"Are you still in foot pursuit?"

"Fuck! Ace, go around the backside!"

I take it as a yes.

Walking through the hallway, the sounds of moans and groans are muffled behind closed doors. Either I've become used to it, or my mind is too focused on what needs to be done for it to only sound like a light buzz in the back of my mind.

"The Mistress isn't seeing anyone right now. Hey!"

Glaring at Jessi, I take the last few steps to the closed door and slam my fist on it a few times.

Knock! Knock knock!

"Come in," Erdene calls out from the other side.

I imagine she enjoys listening to the pounding outside her door.

Twisting the knob, I walk into her office with sure steps. I need fucking answers. I can feel her disgruntled gaze on me as much as I can feel my heart about to beat from my chest. With each step, I get closer to finding out what the hell is going on in this damn house of ill repute.

There is definitely some fucked up shit going on here.

Looking at her evenly, I state the obvious first. "I just took a tour of your basement."

I see a flicker of – well – something before she replies with, "And did you find anything exciting in my basement?" Her attempts to school her features into a bored expression fail. I've been around her too much, I'm already starting to note all her little quirks and manipulations.

"Yeah." I toss what's in my hand toward her. She catches it with quick reflexes and the cogwheel in my mind starts to turn once more. "I found a wedding band."

She doesn't grimace, doesn't change expression - only turns the finger with the ring on it around in her own dainty hands.

"I see," she states.

"Who does it belong to? What the hell is going on in that basement?"

She lets out an exasperated sigh as if this is a fucking game and not like there are severed limbs and appendages scattered about the place in random locations.

"If you must know." I watch as she places the finger on the desk and crosses her arms in front of me, pushing her bosom up. "We handle our business down there with individuals that deserve their punishments."

So she does punish her girls. Filing the information away, I tell myself it's not my business how she disciplines her ladies. "So you're telling me all these missing limbs are because of you?"

Her eyes sparkle and there's a curve to her lip. What does this mean?

"The gift you brought me is because of me. The body you found outside is something else entirely. Have you gotten any farther on that, Mister Reeves?" Her condescending tone grates my nerves and my hands itch to wrap around her neck with all her riddles and play on words.

"I'm doing exactly what you paid me to do. It would help if the ladies of this house would just open their damn mouths and tell me what I need to know!" Never have I found such a tight lipped group of women.

No matter who my men question, it's always the same damn answer.

"We are Eden. The garden flourishes where genesis ends."
What the hell does that fucking mean?

Erdene smiles the longer I stare daggers into her eyes. "Better to direct that anger where it makes a difference, *Cornell.* I have other business to attend to at this very moment."

I'm about to corner her at her desk and tell her what's really on my mind when the radio crackles.

"Boss, we got him." Beau's voice comes in out of breath.

Snarling at the Mistress, her laughter bounces off the walls as I exit her office and out the front door. I'll handle her later.

My boots stomp toward the east side of the building to find one of my men with his knee on the back of some guy on the ground.

"Tell him what you told me, fucker."

"Fuck you!"

Ace twists his arm and we all hear a loud crack right before the guy screams bloody murder. Fuck. Hopefully, this doesn't come back on us. But knowing Ace, he gets off on a good cat and mouse chase. He's too fresh from the field.

"Fucking assholes! I'm going to kill you!"

Thwack!

"Ace! Dammit, man! We need to question the fool before you break his damn jaw!"

Ace grins at the suspect on the ground, his face close enough to rip his ear off. Shit. Now that I'm thinking of it, my feet lead me closer to the two in case he decides to do just that.

Beau stands over them with his arms crossed, laughing like a loon.

"His jaw doesn't need to be fully working for us to get information out."

Shoving Ace off the suspect, I hear him growl but Beau shoves him again with a meaty hand on his chest.

"That's the boss. Don't forget. Get your head together, man."

Growling, Ace bares his teeth at me and stomps off in the other direction. His thirst for blood, evident in his eyes.

Dragging up the suspect, my face is met with a splatter of wetness across my eyes. Fuck! Wiping the blood off with the back of my hand, I throw him down on the ground, letting his head bounce off the concrete.

"Beau, secure him in the basement of the house."

"You got it."

Since the tools are already there, we might as well utilize it.

Dragging his body into the lobby, Jessi huffs but doesn't look startled. I file that fact away in my mind. These ladies don't operate like normal women. All their reactions are out of whack. I feel like the answer I'm seeking is right in front of my face but I still can't put my finger on it. We throw the guy down the stairs and descend slowly. I'm sure these fine ladies can clean up any mess we leave behind. They've done well so far from what I've seen.

Beau grabs the man and slams him onto the table, strapping him down. His good arm flails and his leg kicks out, but one fist to the face stuns him long enough to secure him in place.

"Who the fuck sent you?" Beau snarls.

"Fuc-"

Thwack!

The knuckles on my right hand begin to feel warm with all the work I'm putting them through.

"Beau, grab the tool to the left of you." I tilt my head to let him know it's his turn.

The only thing I get out of this fucker is that he works for someone big and that someone is out to conquer The House of Eden. Memories of that phone call back in Erdene's office come to mind. It has to be him. All the evidence points that direction.

"Do your worst!" The suspect sounds like he's coughing up a bloody lung as Beau does just that.

"Finish up. We need to call in about that dead whore upstairs."

With a nod, the sound of blood curdling screams echo around us. I'm sure the client's upstairs aren't able to decipher if it belongs to one of the girls screaming in pleasure since this guy's tone just went up a few notches as Beau cuts off his balls and shoves them into his mouth to shut him up.

I watch as he shoves the tool into his chest, spraying blood across his face. It doesn't prevent him from smiling as we both stare at the suspect's life leaving his eyes.

How are we going to go about this? From what Jinder tells me, Alexander Jones is a big player in the game of whore houses and trades of the flesh. One simply just doesn't waltz in and shoot him in the head.

Narrowing my eyes on Beau as he twists the scissors into the corpse's body, I ask myself why the hell not?

"Beau, how are your sniper skills?"

"Pffft. I know it's been a damn minute but it's like riding a bicycle. You never truly forget. It's an extension of you."

"I got a job for you."

Beau turns his bloody face and gives me a smile full of crimson teeth.

Smiling back, the familiar feeling of being on a manhunt again increases the blood pumping through my veins. "Seems we got ourselves a rat to catch."

Chapter Twenty-One

ERDENE

Möngömaa's hand is sent to me in a gift-wrapped box. It's been cleaned and frozen, preventing any of the stench from becoming obvious before it arrived at my office.

"Magda, we're going to have to do something about this," I tell her.

"What do you need me to do? Do we even know who hired him?"

"We may have to pay dear old Alexander a visit today. I'll get as much information as I can and distract him. I'm going to need you to tell the girls to question all the patrons that come in. Find out as much as you can."

"Yes, Mistress."

Clicking my tongue, I dismiss her. A breeze comes through, telling me that Magda has exited. Grabbing the phone on my desk, my fingers quickly bring up the number I'm looking for. Hitting the call button, I wait patiently, allowing my mind to relax before answering in the right tone of voice.

"You really think you can just call me after all that's happened?" His annoyed voice comes over the speaker.

My voice purrs. "Alexander. I missed you too."

"You're going to need to erase my number. I'm done with your games, Erdene."

Softly chuckling into the receiver, my mind can already picture a blade in my hand as I slice it across his neck. I may be a woman, but I am not stupid to archaic manipulation tactics like twisting the blame. What is it with men?

"That's fine. Your wife's number was next on my list of people to call. Goodbye, Alexander."

"Fucking cunt! Don't call me, don't call her, don't call any of my establishments. What we have is now over! You hear me? Keep your worthless pussy on your side and never speak to me again."

My lips lift in a snarl, my mind processing the perfect answer when gunshots ring out in the lobby. Hanging up, I quickly run outside to find random men fighting against my own.

Fuck! Alexander just had to draw his hand first.

One of the strangers screams in pain as one of my whores throws a knife into his neck. She's half naked, heaving with her little body full of anger. These men have no idea what they just walked into - a house full of women scorned.

One of the enemies gets thrown my direction by one of my guards and I pull the hair pin out, stabbing him in the eye while he lays on the ground. The blood spurts and lands on my hand, but it also lubricates my weapon enough to easily slip it back out.

"Girls!"

Whores, some in their undergarments come out and join the fray. Magda must have run down to the basement because I can see her pass some of our tools to the other ladies to use as weapons.

The sound of men grunting and fighting makes it hard for me to hear what my girls are yelling but my eyes tell me they're handling themselves just fine.

Someone tries to grab me from behind, but my body reacts by flipping him over and shoving my hair pin up his jaw and into the cavern of his mouth. Slipping out before anyone else can catch me off guard, I run to my car and start the engine with a roar.

Quickly reversing, my tires screech as I slam on the gas and merge onto the main road. The drive to Alexander's personal home only takes about thirty minutes. Whether he's there or not matters none to me. He's hit the only thing I care about and now it's time I take the only thing he cares about.

When the mansion comes into view, I run over his flowers and almost crash into the gardener before I put the vehicle into park. Turning off the engine, I walk toward his front door and turn the knob.

"Pinche, puta! Watch where you're going? What the hell are you doing?" the gardener yells.

"I'm here for a fucking visit. What does it look like I'm doing?"

"You're on private property!"

Ignoring all the voices around me, I continue up the steps.

Of course, rich people wouldn't think to lock their doors when they have workers out in front. Simple minded fools. My heels *click, click, click* on the marble floor and suddenly I'm met with a dainty, well-dressed woman at the top of the steps.

"I'm sorry. Who are you?"

"I'm here to see Alexander. He owes me something." I make sure she gets a good look at me.

Her eyes are blank. She neither frowns or smiles. *Curious.*

"He's not here. He's still at work. Would you like to leave a message with me? I'm his wife."

Oh, I know she is. I've seen her face enough on the screen of his phone when she calls him and tells him how much she misses him. She continues to stand there like an aristocrat, looking down at a peasant and my inner fire burns brighter. Not today. Today we're just going to plant the seed of doubt in Mrs. Jones's mind. Best to let the truths unfold before her very eyes slowly so she can die a slow death on the inside.

"I see. I'll try to catch him at work then. But If I do miss him, please let Alexander know that he missed our appointment today and that he still owes me panties. It was very nice to meet you Mrs. Jones."

Turning, my heels click loudly until I reach the front door and back into my car. Pulling away from his property, I smile to myself as I head toward the whore house I know he frequents the most.

MISTER REEVES

Where the fuck is she?

"Where the hell is your Mistress? Did she not notice the attack right at her fucking doorstep?" I ask anyone and everyone.

None of the women answer. The only sneer at my men as they clean off their makeshift weapons and head back to their rooms like this is an everyday occurrence. What is wrong with this place?

"Ace. Give me updates on Beau's whereabouts."

Ace wipes the blood off his face and blade before speaking into the radio. "Two meters out, waiting for a clear shot."

Good. We need to end this shit once and for all. This was supposed to be a simple security job.

"Get Benson to do a head count on the girls. I need to make a call for a clean up crew."

Six guys. Six well-armed guys, strolled through the front of this place and began shooting. What the hell kind of gang shit can a house full of whores get into? This was planned. Someone thought this through and waited for the right time.

My question is, why wait until the house had guards? Why hasn't this house been hit prior to that?

Hitting the call button on my phone, the blood makes my finger slip. Wiping the screen off on my shirt I hit it again. "Jinder."

"They're already on their way. You're lucky I just came back from a job and saw that shit on time."

"On time, my ass. My men are injured."

"But are any of them dead? No? Then quit complaining. I got five guys coming in. You'll recognize them, they've been on a few missions with you in the past."

"Fuck. This was supposed to be -"

"-A simple security job. Right. Well, once you take your head out of your ass and see reality, you can call me back."

The asshole hangs up on me, the echo of his laugh ringing in my ears.

Shoving my phone into my cargo pocket, I barge into Erdene's office. The first thing I see is an open box. Walking over to it, I curse under my breath and head out the front doors.

"Jessi. Inform me if the Mistress comes back."

She sneers at me but doesn't say no. Her attitude will have to do for now.

Jumping into my vehicle I radio the men. "Send me Beau's location to my phone. I need it in the next two minutes."

"On it."

Ping!

I take a left onto the freeway and let the navigation lead me to my destination.

It's about an hour drive from the House of Eden. The neon lights of the front let everyone in the whole damn town know exactly what kind of establishment this is.

I don't see Erdene's vehicle but I scope the place from where I park anyway. I'm about a few blocks away, looking through my binoculars when the screams start.

Women are running out while men are running in.

"Find the shooter!"

Turning the engine on, I pull out and drive leisurely back toward the freeway.

Chapter Twenty-Two

ERDENE

Alexander didn't even allow me on the premises. It's an embarrassment to be turned away by his men right outside the parking lot. He's going to pay for what he's done. I'm just going to bide my time until he's all but forgotten about me.

I'm sure his wife won't.

Whoever Cornell hired to clean up the place, did a quick job of it. By the time I make it back to the house, the bodies are gone and the lobby smells like bleach. The carpet is replaced, looking glaringly new in a building that's older than I am.

Asking no questions, I walk the halls and speak to my girls one at a time, telling them to gather. None of them know what's going on but everyone is on pins and needles.

"I haven't heard anything, Mistress."

"You know we don't leave the premises."

"Who would want to do this to us?"

Many. Many would want to watch a house of women fall. The naivety of their replies make my gut churn. At this rate, we'll quickly fall victim again. Yes, they are all trained to at least defend themselves and to wield weapons and torture devices in our basement, but the outside world has much more they haven't yet faced.

The previous regime did us harm by locking us away for use.

Am I no better, since they all still choose to remain safe behind our walls after my ascent? I need to increase our numbers back up. That means finding girls from the outside and bringing them in.

"Ladies. A change is going to have to be made."

"What kind of change?"

"There's too many already!"

Glaring at the last voice, she shrinks back behind another girl. I will not tolerate complaints. What must be done will be done.

"We need to initiate more girls into the House of Eden." The silence is deafening. The tension in the room is becoming thick but I ignore it. "Our extracurricular activities are going to have to be put on hold in the meantime. The guards are already questioning us."

"What happens when they find out?"

Turning slowly to Nadya, I speak loudly enough for each of my girls to hear, but quiet enough for the men to not. "All weak links will be eliminated. This is the House of Eden. The birth of snakes and treachery will be removed. The garden flourishes where genesis ends."

All the girls murmur our mantra before we split up and return to our regular duties. Jessi cancels all appointments for the next few hours to allow the women to clean up and ready themselves for servicing.

After all, time is money and we need as much as we can to fortify our home. Another attack like the one today cannot happen again. We are just lucky none of our guards were taken out. But a few of them are missing.

My heels click down the steps and head toward the lobby, the sound muffling from the newly installed carpet. It's blood red, how convenient. As if we are preparing for more bloodshed by our front doors.

"Jessi."

"We will be open to patrons in the next two hours."

"Thank you. I'll be in my office."

"Yes, Mistress."

A hand claps over my mouth the moment the door closes. The sound of the lock turning is loud in my ears. My heart speeds up but I even my breathing, telling myself to take stock of what's happening before making any rash moves.

"I've watched you, you know?" An unrecognizable, masculine voice is husky next to my ears. "The way your ass sways and your head held high with every step you take."

There's a pause in his speech. Does he wish for me to respond... with his hand over my mouth?

"Whores should know their place."

Anticipating death, I bite his hand and head butt him with the back of my skull. *Crunch!* The pain is sharp but my anger is sharper. Swiftly turning, I throw an elbow only to have his bloody smile dodge backward. He's quick, I'll give him that.

His pupils darken right before the smile morphs into a snarl. Ducking his swing, I land on my knees and swiftly take off my heel.

Oof.

His heavy body lands on mine, knocking the wind out of me but I wrestle enough to slip my hand out to impale his temple with the stiletto of my heel.

"You bitch!"

Thwack!

My eyes darken for a second after he lands a fist to my face. My mind floats as if I'm outside of my body. I can feel him pummeling my gut and my face, over and over. The intensity of the pain melts together to create a constant numbness in my skull and ribs.

A new growl joins us and it sounds so far away. Suddenly, I feel like I'm floating. When my mind finally comes back to reality, the sound of flesh-on-flesh drifts to my ears reminding me of the debauchery we serve here. What is happening? Masculine grunts and growls ebb and flow until there's a loud crash right next to my head. The splinters and shrapnel of wood lodge themself into the meaty part of my face.

I think I hear pounding on the wall, but my mind is fighting hard to not drift in and out of consciousness.

With what strength I have, I crawl and pull my body to the far side of the room, groaning in pain as I push myself to a sitting position, facing my desk. My vision is blurry, both from tears and from how puffy my eyes have become. Blinking rapidly, my head feels like it wants to split in two before I finally force my eyes to the sight before me.

My desk is broken right down the middle. The computer has become a casualty in the fight.

Mister Reeves lays on his back on the floor, holding what looks like a wound to his liver.

A deep groan escapes him as he tries to move. No sound comes from the other figure, his body looks mangled, some of his limbs bent the wrong direction.

Yet, the only thing that intensifies my already pounding headache is the fact that I'm going to need to replace my computer.

"Celia." Mister Reeves' raspy voice breaks the silence.

Letting my head fall back against the wall, I close my eyes.

"I got him, Celia. I got him."

Who's he talking about? Who's he talking to?

One thing I hate getting used to is the sound of the death rattle - the final breath before death's embrace.

It's the only thing I hear until my mind drifts back from the darkness.

Another crash startles me awake and suddenly the room is full of voices. It feels like knives in the back of my eyes and skull every time a new voice drifts through.

"Call an ambulance! Now!"

"Magda! Let Isla do it, she's faster!"

The shouts start to sound muffled, and my body feels heavy, each breath causing pain in my chest. So. Much. Pain.

Memories of my first few weeks in the House of Eden become lullabies as darkness finally consumes me.

Chapter Twenty-Three

MAGDA

Erdene has been put on bed rest since her exit from the house. No one knows how long her recovery will take or if she's going to make it at all.

Beau stepped up as head of security while I stepped up as Mistress. Jessi doesn't agree with the decision, but majority vote rules. With Möngömaa gone, I'm one of the longest standing whores left.

The men inform us of their burial of Mister Reeves, but none of us know him well enough to want to attend. We didn't even get a chance to attend any of the deaths of our missing girls. Their limbs still scattered in undisclosed locations.

The only thing left of Erdene and her reign here are the security, the new carpet, and her car.

The only problem with this dynamic is that none of us know how to drive, so the vehicle is pointless to us.

Ace offered his service but ended up taking too much from one of our girls as payment. Now we have another girl recovering in her room and a new tension between us and the men sworn to look over us.

We're walking victims to the outside world, and we know it. We were never privy to who Erdene's outside contact is for our extracurricular activities, so now we can't even bring in extra cash for that.

"I compiled a list of girls we recruited for the house of Eden." Jessi's voice breaks me from my thoughts of the future.

"How many girls do we have?"

"Five."

That's barely enough to cover the bodies we've lost.

"What are we doing with our current guards?"

"You're the Mistress. What do you want us to do?"

"Some of them are unhinged. Their eyes speak of all the things they've wanted to do to us for so long. With Mister Reeves gone, I don't trust them. Beau is the only semi decent one, even so, I still don't trust that gleam in his eye when I walk by."

"What would you have me do?"

Running my hands through my hair with my elbows on my knees, I sit on Erdene's bed, wanting to bury myself alive instead of being in this position. We've gained so much with Erdene, now we've gone back to zero.

"We need to start again, just like we're doing with the girls. It's the only way."

Nodding, Jessi stands up and leaves, softly shutting the door behind her.

I sit up and let my body fall back onto the sheets. What a fucking mess this is.

The only other option for income are the jars in the basement. I wonder how the black market is going.

～

"Alright ladies, welcome to the House of Eden. We have simple rules here. Do as you're told, perform your jobs well, and make sure to never perpetuate the sins of our mothers and fathers. Children will not be tolerated here, do you understand?"

The new girls nod as the old crew takes in our recent addition. The initial five girls integrated well. This new batch will have to go through our trial period like everyone else.

"Mark, make sure you escort our new ladies to their rooms."

"Yes, Mistress." Our new head of security obediently follows orders.

The old guards made their departure difficult. Mostly Ace, who had his eye on Nadya like a meal. I was lucky enough to have stored away Mister Reeves cell phone before the authorities came through.

There was only one number on it. Without Jinder, we would have never been able to get rid of the old guard and find replacements.

I still owe payment for the next year.

He's just lucky he's skilled with his cock.

Smiling at the memory of our last fight and the way he subdued me, I turn to my recent five and loudly voice our mantra.

"What are we ladies?"

In unison, we repeat what we've all been taught since Erdene's rule. "We are Eden. The garden flourishes where genesis ends."

"Good. Patrons are scheduled to come in within the next thirty minutes. Get yourselves ready."

"Yes, Mistress," they say in unison.

Watching my ladies head to their designated rooms, I pat Jessi on the shoulder before heading back to my office.

"Let me know if anything pops up."

"Yes, Mistress."

Entering the door, I softly shut it behind me and walk past the new small desk we were given. A new state of the art computer fits on the surface, and I shake my head at how big the damn computer screen is.

Turning the knob to the back bedroom door, something warm and hard slams into my back before the sound of the door slamming reaches my ears.

Not again.

A quick elbow, twist and knee up puts me face to face with dark eyes and a devilish smile. Jinder easily counters all my moves right before his hand grips my neck and walks me backward until I fall onto the sheets.

His mouth slams on mine without removing his hand. His thumb caresses my chin with a false sense of security. I never know which Jinder I get. Sometimes he wants to kill me, sometimes he wants to purge his inner demons into my pussy.

"Magda."

How does he expect me to talk with his tongue down my throat?

He chuckles, knowing exactly what he's doing.

"I've been on edge lately, the bloodlust not doing its job." He sucks in my bottom lip, giving me room to finally take a breath in. "But lucky for me, it's payday."

Epilogue

KATELYN

I t's as if nothing happened.

The audacity of these whores is unreal.

My eyes can still feel my brother's presence here, his death unjustified, despite the fact that I wasn't here to witness it. My twin brother and I have a deep connection like that, it's beyond this life.

If only he finished the job the way he was supposed to. The fool. Always so hardheaded. Always running away from me when all I wanted to do was love him.

He should have just killed the head whore to begin with, like he was paid to do. Instead, he has to play around with her second.

Fucking asshole!

My jealousy rises but I school my features. The man above me continues to thrust, his gasps and groans reminding me of swine. He snorts and my lip curls out of his view.

Groaning over me, I thank the lord he's practically a five-pump chump.

Cooing in his ear, I bite his lobe, and caress his hair.

"That's a good boy. You like cumming inside of me, don't you? You like the way you fill me up, dripping out my cunt."

He groans again and pumps a few more times despite his small dick already beginning to shrink.

Mister Williams' kink is praise. Apparently, his small dick doesn't impress the ladies and it's eating away at his ego. The House of Eden is his solution and his entrapment because he can never face the real world anymore. Not when the House caters to his every desire.

I just wish he'd fuck a different whore.

He grunts when his dick fully slips out and stands up to get dressed. The only good thing about this encounter is that he's quick and leaves a sizable tip because he only wants me.

If only my twin, Jack, wanted me like this. My eyes burn with anger and jealousy over the fact he fucked that whore's corpse before he sent her severed hand to the queen whore.

When all he had to do was come back home to me!

"Thank you, my dear. Until our next visit."

Staring at the back of Mister Williams, I smile, but my mind is still in chaos over my loss. It doesn't matter if it's been a year. It still feels like yesterday when my world turned upside down and the news report mentioned my brother's name on TV as one of the victims at the house.

I told Jack I would handle Alexander! The fool never would listen and now he's six feet under. Without me! Leaving me in so much fucking misery that I can't even enjoy the fact that someone sniped dear 'ol husband.

It was perfect! Our hands would have been clean, Jack! How could you?

I knew what I had to do the moment that whore entered my home. It was easy becoming one of them. I'm surprised none of the other brothels have taken them over.

Grinning to myself, I count the cash and place it in the safe behind the dresser.

Knock knock!

"It's open!"

The guard that stands outside my door grins as he opens the door per the rules of the house. It lets everyone know my pussy is open for service once again.

"Thank you." I've mastered the art of pleasantries and false masks while living with Alexander.

The guard smiles and sneaks a look at my naked breasts before turning around to leave and check on the other girls.

That's right. Keep your smiles. Let them all smile. Soon they will all feel the wrath of my broken heart, one severed limb at a time.

About Emery LeeAnn

Emery LeeAnn is an International Best Selling Author who lives in Ohio with her family.

Besides being addicted to coffee, she is a true believer that variety adds spice to your life. Writing in every genre gives her the variety she craves.

Her characters like to invade her mind every hour of the day, usually waking her up in the middle of the night.

Loving the dark and gray side of things, she is exploring her passion with the written word. There are many wonders to come from her in her twisted Wonderland..... Stick around, you may find you enjoy her special brand of torture.

https://linktr.ee/EmeryLeeann
For updates on Emery, check out the link below for access to her groups, website, newsletter & author pages!

If you get your kicks in a magical manner, order toys from websites like bad dragon, and prefer your monsters *in* your bed instead of *under* them, then Y. D. is your girl.

Writing everything from spicy dark fantasy to fluffier-than-a-cool-marshmallow romance, Y.D. La Mar has her fingers in all sorts of man-meat pie, and the sky is the limit. Somehow, this magical mistress manages to balance her spicy author life with her responsibilities as a mom, a wife, and a resident of Sin City *—oh, irony, you've felled me.*

When the world is full of black-and-white, Y.D. plays in the grey zones, spending her time creating new ways to shock and awe her editor, as well as her readers.

Follow Me!

Want updates and sneak peeks?

Sign up for my newsletter!

Also by YD La Mar

STREET ARRHYTHMIA TRILOGY

The Scent of Jasmine

For The Love of Import & Blood

To The Beat of The Streets

Spinoff

Arachnophilia

REVERSE HAREM

Warring Suns

SCI FI

The Essence of Esme

PARANORMAL

The Hunger of Thieves

Heart of The Reaper

Heart of the Reaper: Tales from the Underworld

Soul of The Reaper

Fate of The Reaper

Bury Me Alive

Lead Me Through The Fire

PSYCHOLOGICAL THRILLER

The Truth Enslaved

CONTEMPORARY

The Formation of Us

The Conception of Us

The Revelation of Us

The House of Eden (cowrite)

When the Bloom Burns (cowrite)

OMEGAVERSE

Gero

Bernhard

Severin

DYSTOPIAN/POST APOCALYPTIC

We Are the Fallen

MONSTER SHORT STORIES

Sinful Attraction

The Sky Below

Maeonia

Between Heaven and Earth

Fantasies Inflamed

Her 13th Hour

Ignus Fatuus

ANTHOLOGIES

Used and Bound

Captured by Darkness

Until the End

After the Rain

Into The Woods

A Foster Fling

Bound by Monsters

Once Upon a Nightmare

Monsters in Love: Lost in the Dark

Monsters in Love: Lost in the Forest

Monsters in Love: Monstrous Ever After

Monsters in Love: Lost in the Deeps

Monsters in Love: Aloha Nui Loa

Pollinators

The Red Key Club: Valentines Day Edition

The Red Key Club: Halloween Edition

Creepy Court

Crimson Vendetta

For the Love of Villains

SHARED WORLDS

Inferno World

Games of the Underworld

Rise of the Dreads

Monsters Ball

Rescue Me: A Hero Romance Collection